ONCE MORE WITH CHUTZPAH

ONCE MORE WITH CHUTZPAH

HALEY NEIL

BLOOMSBURY
NEW YORK LONDON OXFORD NEW DELHI SYDNEY

BLOOMSBURY YA
Bloomsbury Publishing Inc., part of Bloomsbury Publishing Plc
1385 Broadway, New York, NY 10018

BLOOMSBURY and the Diana logo are trademarks of Bloomsbury Publishing Plc

First published in the United States of America in February 2022 by Bloomsbury YA

Bloomsbury books may be purchased for business or promotional use.
For information on bulk purchases please contact Macmillan Corporate and
Premium Sales Department at specialmarkets@macmillan.com

Library of Congress Cataloging-in-Publication Data
Names: Neil, Haley, author.
Title: Once more with chutzpah / by Haley Neil.
Description: New York : Bloomsbury Children's Books, 2022.
Summary: Anxious eighteen-year-old Tally and her twin, Max, set off on a high school
exchange trip to Israel, where she explores her Jewish heritage, mental health struggles,
and sexual and romantic identity.
Identifiers: LCCN 2021018086 (print) | LCCN 2021018087 (e-book)
ISBN 978-1-5476-0709-9 (hardcover) • ISBN 978-1-5476-0777-8 (e-book)
Subjects: CYAC: Jews—Fiction. | Israel—Fiction. | Identity—Fiction. | Brothers and
sisters—Fiction. | Twins—Fiction. | Voyages and travels—Fiction.
Classification: LCC PZ7.1.N3965 On 2022 (print) | LCC PZ7.1.N3965 (e-book) |
DDC [Fic]—dc23
LC record available at https://lccn.loc.gov/2021018086
LC e-book record available at https://lccn.loc.gov/2021018087

Book design by Jeanette Levy
Typeset by Westchester Publishing Services
Printed and bound in the U.S.A.
2 4 6 8 10 9 7 5 3 1

To find out more about our authors and books visit
www.bloomsbury.com and sign up for our newsletters.

For Mom and Dad,
But Mom more
(because she said so)

ONCE
MORE WITH
CHUTZPAH

OPENING UP

If I were to pick the starting point for an epic adventure, it definitely wouldn't be the Dine Express in Logan Airport, Terminal C. We're sitting four to a table clearly meant for two, the black surface almost completely hidden under sandwich wrappers and cups and bags of chips. There isn't much space at the pre-security airport café, but we're making it work.

Mom clears her throat. "Babies," she starts, holding up her drink like she's about to make a toast.

"Technically adults now," I interrupt. Max and I have been eighteen for a full month, so it counts.

"My little infants," she continues, "you are about to embark on a spiritual journey. One that will change you irrevocably. We send you off as children and expect you to return with aged souls, lightened by the wisdom you gather on your great adventure."

"Lizzie, they'll be gone for less than two weeks," Dad says. "I just hope they return without sunburns."

"I'm excited for them," Mom says. "It's been a couple of years since I've been to Israel for a conference."

One thing about having a mother who is a religious studies professor is that her business trips are to places like Jerusalem. Add that to the fact that Dad spent every summer growing up visiting family in Tel Aviv, and it all becomes pretty awful that Max and I haven't been to Israel yet. We're the only two in our family who still need to go.

I take the last sip of my drink. "We should probably find our group," I say. We were greeted at the El Al check-in by our trip coordinator, who handed us name tags and told us we were a half hour too early.

Dad nods as though I've just said something very sage. "Time to fly the nest," he says.

"We *are* coming back," I point out.

"Then off to college next year," Mom adds.

Hopefully, I think. I look over at Max, who is silently picking at the excess bread from his sandwich, a tiny pile of crumbs accumulated on the plastic wrapper. If everything goes as planned, he'll be a lot happier when we get back—maybe even happy enough to apply to Boston University like we planned.

We clean up before Mom and Dad walk us to the El Al check-in. "This is where we leave you," Dad says. "Love you, baby girl."

"Love you, Daddio," I say.

Mom wraps me in a big hug and whispers, "Keep an eye on your brother."

I nod, my chin hitting her shoulder.

She pulls away and gives my arm a squeeze. "Have the best time."

I take out the name tag we got when we arrived at the airport, big and plastic with a blue-and-white lanyard, and put it around my neck.

Let's do this.

After we say goodbye, Max and I walk toward the check-in counter. There's a small line, partitioned off by a black divider. When we get to the front, two spots open. I walk one way; Max walks the other.

I approach a man with an El Al Airlines pin on his collar and a thick black beard. He's looking at a clipboard. "Name?" he asks without looking up.

"Tally," I say. "Talia. Talia Gelmont, I mean."

"Age?" he asks.

"Eighteen."

"Passport?"

"Yes, I have one," I say.

At this, he looks up, vaguely annoyed. "Here?"

I rummage through my carry-on. I put my passport right in the front pocket with the packing instruction guide our group sent us, but we haven't even reached security, so I didn't think I would need it yet.

"Here," I say, handing over my passport. As he examines it, I worry that I don't look enough like my passport picture.

I shouldn't have straightened my hair for the photo. Or worn it down in the first place. I should have known better; I should have—

I catch myself starting to spiral and take a deep breath. A full-blown panic attack requires at least four symptoms. Heart racing, shortness of breath. That's two. I'm not dissociating and I'm not dizzy and I don't have any chest pain. I feel only the regular sense of both doom and gloom, so that barely counts.

The check-in guy flips through the blank pages of my passport. "Never traveled?"

"Not out of the country, no." Is this a good thing? A bad thing? An embarrassing thing?

"To confirm, you have never been to Iran, Iraq, Syria, Lebanon, Egypt?"

Just Arabic countries? Well, that's high-key racist.

"No, I have not been out of the country."

But Max has traveled outside the country before, which probably means that this trip is ruined. He should have never gone to that gifted program in Madrid two summers ago.

My anxiety is watching my carefully curated plan crumble to the ground.

I look over at him. He's standing with another employee, in the middle of his very own interrogation. He looks normal—hair too long and puffy, wearing an oversize sweatshirt he stole from our dad. I can't see the scar from this angle, though I know that it's still curved over his left eyebrow. He almost looks the way he did before the crash, before he became something fragile.

4

Mr. Beard hands me back my passport.

He continues to ask me questions, ranging from whether or not anyone asked me to bring any packages to Israel to details about my family in Tel Aviv. Logic brain knows this has only been a few minutes, but anxiety brain is telling me that we've been talking for five hours and I will never get on that plane and might end up in jail, probably, for no discernible reason.

"Is there anything you think you should tell me?" he finally asks.

Yes, frightening beard man. I would like to say you're freaking me out with these questions, and they seem extremely unnecessary when I'm about to hand over my suitcase and go through a metal detector.

Which I shouldn't say out loud.

"Nope. Nothing comes to mind."

The man waves to the check-in counter behind him. "Drop off your suitcase there. Enjoy Israel."

"You too!" I reply and then immediately realize what I have just said. "If you're going as well? And, um. Thank you? For protecting, uh . . . You said over here?" I point directly behind me to the suitcase scale/counter with El Al above it. "Okay, thanks!"

Mr. Beard is noticeably not listening to me, as he has now moved on to the next person in line.

I drop off my suitcase, which is thankfully the right amount of heavy for an international flight, and get my boarding pass. Max is already standing off to the side of the check-in counter, ticket in hand.

"So are you a risk to Israeli society?" he asks.

"I'm apparently a risk to society at large, but there's really no helping me now." I adjust the strap on my carry-on bag. "Did they ask you about traveling to Arabic countries?"

"Yeah. Felt very wrong," Max says.

I nod, then wave toward security. "All right, come on, Moxie."

"After you, Tallytubby," he says.

So I take the lead.

ON MY OWN

Max and I walk toward the security line. It's not too long; I've seen far worse for Thanksgiving travel to visit Safta and Sabba in Florida. I guess I thought it might be different with us going abroad. The check-in people have already basically grilled us; the security officers probably don't need to do much more.

I look back to where my parents were standing when we walked to the check-in desk, but they're already gone. I don't know what I thought they would do. Wait until we were officially past security and therefore inaccessible? Stay in the airport the whole time?

There's something jarring about their absence. Something that makes it official. Max and I are really going to Israel. Alone.

I rub the bead on my fidget ring.

"You okay?" Max asks.

"Yeah, I just . . . I can't remember whether I need to take this off," I say, twisting the ring.

Max shrugs. "I already took off my jewelry, just to avoid that very problem."

A joke. He said it deadpan, without the usual lightness he uses to tease me, but it's a start.

Security goes pretty quickly. Max spends most of his time looking at his phone, and I spend most of my time looking at everyone around us. I'm trying to figure out where people are going, coming up with imaginary background stories. The man with the yarmulke on top of his head is probably on his way to Israel just like we are; the mother and daughter talking rapidly in French are headed to Paris to visit family. I've just decided that one woman in front of us in line is an international spy when I see a girl with a lanyard just like ours.

I hit Max's arm.

He looks up, annoyed. "Yes?"

"There's someone with a lanyard. We should introduce ourselves."

"How?" he asks, looking over to where I'm pointing. "They're way ahead of us."

"Well, when the line loops over, we can just—"

"Why don't we get through security first. Then we'll make introductions," he says.

I frown. Fine, we can start making friends at the gate.

Except Max is a dirty liar, because when we get to the gate, he sits down in one of those uncomfortable airport seats, puts on his headphones—the big noise-canceling ones he got last year to edit music and play video games—and starts watching something on his phone. By now, there are tons of other people around with name tags on. So many people, in fact, I think there must be a few different tour groups all heading out on the same flight.

I sit down in the seat next to him and lift a speaker off one ear. "Shouldn't we try to find other people who are in our group now?" I ask.

"I would," he starts, "but I *did* already start this episode of *The Nanny* . . ."

I let go of the headphone so it snaps against the side of his head.

This is fine. This will definitely be fine. The trip hasn't even really started; we're still in Massachusetts. There are so many people here anyway; not everyone will even be on our trip. Sure, Max has been spending the last few . . . months, really, alone in his room, but once we're there, he'll have to be social. There's no way to be a loner when you're crammed on a bus with thirty teenagers, driving around a new country.

When I found out that our local temple youth group was organizing a joint high school exchange trip to Israel with a few other nearby congregations, I knew I had found the perfect solution. The old Max thrived on social interactions. This has got to spark something in him. I think about his guitar, sitting untouched in our basement back home. Maybe all the social energy will even get him to compose a song. He used to love doing that.

A song. I take out my notebook from my purse. I guess I could try writing now, since we're apparently not making friends until the plane touches down.

My love for musicals started when I was little and my parents took me and Max to see a local production of *Wicked*. Honestly, that was it; I was hooked. I couldn't get over the songs, the way the lyrics twisted together to tell the story. You could say that something had changed within me . . . something was not the same. I went through a phase where I watched nothing but movie musicals; I'm talking *Hairspray*, *Grease*, basically 75 percent of all Disney movies. If it had music in it, I would watch, sitting there in front of the screen singing terribly along.

Then in middle school, my best friend, Cat, and I took a trip to visit her nai nai and ye ye in New York. On the second night, her grandparents took us to see the musical *Waitress* on Broadway, famous largely because the music and lyrics were written by the absolute genius songwriter Sara Bareilles. Basically, there's a waitress who is in an unhappy, emotionally abusive marriage. She gets pregnant and then has an affair with her doctor, which is a pretty scandalous plot, considering who we were with. I had never gone through anything even remotely similar to the events in the musical, but I related so deeply to the *feelings* behind the words.

I wanted to *be* Sara Bareilles. If I could ever write anything as moving as "You Matter to Me" or "She Used to Be Mine," then maybe I could make a lasting difference. Maybe I could inspire another person, make them feel whole.

That was when I started writing seriously. Cat would help me figure out the melodies, and on a couple of occasions, we even roped Max in to adding real music to my lyrics. It was just something fun we did, a bonus way to spend our time. Until I got absolutely smacked with writer's block.

I tap my pen against the blank page on the notebook. It looks . . . empty. Daunting even? Which is so supremely ridiculous. I've done this before. I logically know how to do this.

You just need . . . words. Arranged in different ways. And there are letters in those words. I know my letters. I've known my letters for years.

Ugh.

I don't even have a topic I want to write about. That would probably help. But it's hard to focus on writing new songs when you're desperately trying to get your brother back on track.

Because the thing is . . . Max almost died six months ago.

He went to a party, and it was getting late, so he hitched a ride. He didn't know that the driver had been drinking. I didn't know this at the time either. I mean, I knew there was a party and that he was going, but I had a very serious date with the movie musical *The Last Five Years* and a mud mask. But then I got the call.

No one calls on the house phone unless they're a telemarketer or a grandparent, and in both cases, my dad is usually the one to answer. I was the only one home that night since my parents go on these date nights every week because they apparently still love each other, which is both gross and adorable. So there I was, face damp from washing off the mask, rocking some unreasonably old plaid shorts and a tank top when the phone started to ring. I let it ring once, but by the second ring, I had convinced myself that it was probably just Safta trying to figure out how to use the microwave again, and I would be a bad granddaughter if I didn't answer.

It happened two streets away; he was almost home. I ran. I ran in those old shorts and the tank top and a pair of my dad's too-big sneakers that were right by the door. I can't drive and it was so close and I had to be there. He was lying in the back of an ambulance when I arrived. His left eye was puffy and covered in blood.

"She's gone, Tal," he said. His voice sounded like everything had been sapped out of it. Quiet and blank, he continued. "I saw her. She's gone. She's really gone."

Just like that, Max became the boy who watched a classmate die.

It seemed like our whole town went into mourning. *Only seventeen, so young, so tragic*, snippets of sadness passed between grocery store aisles and over cups of tea.

I know I was supposed to feel the same way, but there was this anger settled in the pit of my stomach that I couldn't shake. How could someone be so reckless? How the hell could anyone get behind the wheel drunk in this freaking day and age? How dare she do that to Max.

There were also whispers about my brother. *That's him,*

the boy who was there. Watched it all, the poor thing. That's what he was now. A poor thing.

When he got back from the hospital with two broken ribs and stitches over his eyebrow, he was supposed to be healing. But he started staying up all night, sleeping during the day. He left the house exactly three times the rest of the summer, and two of those times were to go to the doctor's office. He went eleven days without changing out of the same pair of ratty pajamas. When senior year started, he didn't go back for the first two weeks.

Which was bad enough, but then he missed the BU early application deadline.

We had always planned on applying early to BU. Always. It made the most sense. BU is an amazing school, and with Mom's teaching position there, we'd only have to pay for things like room, board, and books. Not even room and board if we decided to commute, though we'd probably go for dorms, at least at first, to get the full college experience. A full college experience at an amazing discount. And applying early gives you a better chance of getting in.

Max didn't apply early.

It's not like he didn't know it was happening. I was extremely vocal about the deadlines, mostly in the form of loud complaints and constant updates on my own application. When I was finally ready to hit Submit, I went to Max first.

"Want to apply at the same time? We can get Dad to film it; he'll be all emotional."

"I'm not applying," he said.

"And I'm not listening to the *Hadestown* soundtrack tonight. See, we can both be funny."

"Tally, I'm not applying," he repeated.

That's when it became serious. Because while I understood that he was grieving, giving up on a basically guaranteed future was absolutely unacceptable.

I tried to help him feel better. I invited over his friends from his old middle school band and arranged family outings to bowl and play mini golf. I spent two weeks writing motivational quotes on the bathroom mirror. I bought him three different self-help books and left them neatly stacked on the corner of his bed. I baked his favorite chocolate cookies and put together a family game night with his favorite board game, a weird electronic version of Life.

Nothing worked.

The regular decision deadline for BU is two days after we get back from this trip. If he wants to apply, he's going to need to fill out the application and write an essay and then write supplemental essays on top of that. The small blessing here is that we took the SATs together last spring. If he has any chance of getting everything else done now, he has to start while we're on the trip.

This plan has to work; this has to make him feel better. I'm running out of time.

I glance over at Max. He isn't even smiling while he watches *The Nanny*. That's basically the loudest cry for help possible.

I put my notebook back in my purse and take out my earbuds. They're cheaper than Max's but far more practical; two people can listen. I wave them in my brother's face.

Without saying a word, he unplugs his headphones, takes my pair of earbuds, and plugs them in.

We watch together until it's time to board our flight.

DEFYING GRAVITY

Grouping a bunch of young adults on a "life-changing" trip is going to lead to some relationships. Probably friendships, maybe more. It's like if you leave theater kids alone with a piano: at least someone is going to sing. Or hook up. Usually both.

I didn't initially intend for this to play any part in my plan to fix Max. Said plan was mostly to surround him with people, go on Israeli adventures, and cross my fingers that all of that was enough to make him return to normal. At which point I would subtly slide in and say something like, "Oh, hey, the BU deadline is coming up. Might want to work on that." He'd be eternally grateful that I saved his future.

When a girl around our age literally falls into Max's lap on the airplane, I start to reconsider.

"I'm so sorry; this is absurdly embarrassing," she says, standing up. She's got on a trip lanyard with a name tag that reads SAMANTHA LEVINSON. "I tripped over a bag and just," she continues. "Such a great way to start out this trip."

"No, no. Don't worry about it," Max says.

"I'm actually—this is actually my seat," she says, voice apologetic, pointing to the spot next to Max. "Are you here with the Temple Beth El Youth Group?"

"Yeah," he says, holding out his own lanyard. I swear his voice sounds like the beginning of a rom-com, the optimistic and giddy sort. "I'm Max."

"Tally," I say.

"Sammy," she responds. "I'm so excited. I just know we're all going to have so much fun."

"I think we will," Max says. Then he smiles. I missed his smile.

"Which temple do you guys go to?" Sammy asks. "I don't think I've seen you at Temple Beth El."

She hasn't. I can't even remember the last time we went to services. Maybe the High Holidays a couple of years ago? I only found out about this trip because my mom was asked to speak to the congregation as a part of this lecture series, and I tagged along.

That's probably a bad thing. She's going to think we're not Jewish enough to be here.

I hate that *prove you're enough* mindset. Our dad, who is Jewish, and our mom, who is Catholic, tried raising us pretty evenly in both their traditions when we were younger. It gets even more complicated what with the whole *mother who is literally a doctor of religion* thing. Because, for fun, she likes practicing her lectures over the dinner table sometimes (though I'm not sure she's actually aware that's what she's doing), so I can probably school undergrads on rabbinical laws and trends in early Judaic customs, but I never had a bat mitzvah. Sometimes it all messes with my own brain.

"Oh, well, we're interfaith," I answer. "Went to midnight mass the other night. Which is not what you asked. Went to a whole bunch of bar and bat mitzvahs, so."

My rambling doesn't seem to bother Sammy. "You said you're interfaith? What's the other religion?"

"Catholic," I say. Though Mom's ties to Catholicism are pretty loose at this point, seeing as the whole time we were at church with her side of the family, she spent the service muttering about historical inaccuracies.

Max saves me from further embarrassment. "We go to Temple Beth Israel."

"Oh, cool, I've gone to some services there. It's beautiful."

Should I agree with her? Or perhaps go through a detailed list of every single time I've set foot in the building?

"I'm going to run to the bathroom before we take off," Max says, breaking my thought spiral. He stands. "Be right back."

As soon as he's gone, Sammy turns to me. "He's cute," she says, her voice the volume of a stage whisper.

"Oh, uh—he's twin. Max brother. No—" I pause. "Max is my brother," I finally get out. Nailed it.

Her face almost instantly turns red. "I thought you were just temple friends. I'm doing a really great job at making good impressions with your family," she says.

I laugh. "No, don't worry. I'll never tell him; it would go straight to his head."

Straight to his head, I think. Wait. A few years ago, Max found out that Alyssa Greenburg had a crush on him, and he was insufferable, constantly showing off. He wrote her three songs and then applied to that gifted program in Madrid just so he'd seem like a world traveler.

His complete inability to deal with romance could work in my favor now. If he thinks that Sammy likes him, he'll start acting more like himself. He'd probably be so embarrassed if she ever found out about this whole *didn't apply to schools* thing.

And if not, at least he'd make a friend. I try to casually duck out of the conversation when he gets back. I'll let them bond a little now, so it will feel even more meaningful when I let it slip that she likes him.

I take out my notebook and place it on the seat-back tray in front of me just in case inspiration decides to strike on this here flight.

I run my hand over the indents on the notebook, small musical notes patterned across the soft faux leather. It was a gift from Cat. For the last few years, she has given Max and me matching, often ridiculous gifts. Once she bought us both these big makeup sets, the kind I have to assume professional makeup artists use, and then watched gleefully as Max unwrapped his present. Another year, she bought tickets for all three of us to see *Disney on Ice: Frozen*.

Last year's gifts were more practical. She bought us each custom music notebooks, the exterior designed to look like sheet paper. She claimed it was so Max could write *more of his moody nonsense* and so I could write a Tony Award winner.

The obvious thing to do when you can't seem to write any of your own lyrics is to listen to preexisting hits. I start with *Hamilton*. Max and Sammy are still talking. Then I try *Rent*.

It's extremely difficult to go to sleep on a plane. It's harder when people are singing about going out tonight. I switch over to Disney piano music, because I should probably try to get some rest now, and even that's a bust.

Max and Sammy have actually gone to sleep, but at this point, I've given up hope of getting any rest. I try out the airplane entertainment . . . then I try out some airplane food . . . then I give *Wicked* a shot.

I'm not sure if I fall asleep or if I was just imagining myself as Elphaba really hard, but all of a sudden, they're announcing over the loudspeakers that everyone needs to get in their seats and fasten their seat belts. I picture us crashing, but only briefly.

I do a quick check. No physical symptoms of a panic attack. This is just my regular, underlying anxiety, which is fine. I wonder, if the plane was actually about to smash into the ground or spontaneously combust, what I would want to think about. Which might be kind of morbid, but sometimes I think about that, what my last thought should be. Even before Max almost died. Like if I'm crossing the street or in a crowded elevator that's probably too full.

Cat. I think I'd want to picture Cat.

We're starting the descent. I look out the window, and everything seems so small. I always bully my way into getting the window seat. I mean, I don't travel a ton, just to visit Safta and Sabba in their new condo in Sarasota and that trip I took with Cat's family last spring to LA, but those were all within the continental US. This looks different. Tiny greens and fields and scattered houses with red roofs and buildings painted over with washes of tan, like someone took a whole set of toys and brought them to the beach. From this height, everything looks vaguely fake and manufactured. I imagine removing that car or those houses from some ridiculously complicated set of packaging and setting them out to play.

Everything below is getting bigger, and it seems more real, fit for actual people and not just dolls. I think that maybe Israel is not that different from back home. I still see buildings and roads. We're getting closer and closer to a city, those buildings now crammed next to one another.

I stare out the window for the rest of the trip, watching everything grow. Then I see the landing strip. If we were going to crash, it would probably be now, I think, so I imagine Cat, sprawled at the end of my bed as we binge-watch TV, looking back to make sure I'm laughing when she does.

Welcome to Israel.

START OF SOMETHING NEW

"Temple Beth El Youth Group? High school exchange trip?" This too-tall boy is standing just outside the gate as we all get off the plane. His whole body looks lost, voice questioning, thick eyebrows furrowed over his muddy brown eyes.

"Do you need help?" I ask, because sleep-deprived me is apparently a martyr.

He nods, an enthusiastic nod that shakes the dark curls on top of his head.

I enact the Three Easy Rules for Gathering a Large Group of People. 1. Whistle like a soccer coach trying to round up a group of five-year-olds after their very first practice. 2. Delegate tasks. 3. Count heads. I feel like I'm back in the middle of play practice.

Which is how we find out that we're missing two people.

Max, who I gave the task of gathering up stragglers,

walks ahead to investigate, leaving me with a bunch of strangers.

Tall Boy leans over and whispers, "Thanks. It's my first time as a Madrich. There's supposed to be another group leader here, and she's been a Madricha three times already. She's meeting us outside security."

"No worries," I say. I have no idea what a Madrich or a Madricha is, but it sounds official.

"I'm David." He smiles and looks down. For a second, I think he's checking out my chest before I remember I have on a name tag. "Nice to meet you, Talia Gelmont."

"Tally," I correct.

"Nice to meet you, *Tally*." He says my name like it's something special. It's the same way I say *latkes* or *cookie dough*.

"So . . . ," I say. "You're, like, our leader. Captain of the Jew Team."

"I think you're more of the leader right now," he says with a laugh. "I'm just sort of a helper. Keep us together, make sure no one gets lost. Our tour guide is the one in charge."

I look at him. Sure, he's tall, a few inches over six feet, I'd guess, but there's something about his face that seems distinctly young. Less like a grown-up and more like a potential chem partner. "How old are you?" I ask.

"Nineteen. I'm a freshman. I was supposed to be on break, but my mom thought this would be a better use of my time. Said it was a good way to reconnect to the temple. She correctly assumed I wasn't going at school," he explains. "You?"

"Eighteen." I wonder if I should add that I'm a senior? He talked about school. I mean, he has to already know I'm in high school, since I'm on this trip.

"First time in Israel?" he asks.

"First time abroad. You?"

"Oh, I'm a traveler." He actually puffs up his chest with that. "Went on Birthright last summer. There's a big Yemenite Jewish population here, so my grandparents were basically over the moon about it. Went on a family trip to Scotland. Moved on to bigger and better things." He waves his clipboard for emphasis.

"I can see."

A thought flashes through my mind faster than Daveed Diggs's Lafayette rap in "Guns and Ships." Is this flirting? The easy back-and-forth, the tone of voice. *You literally just met him; cool the bleep down*, I tell myself. Because I do this all the time: get fleeting crushes on people without anything ever happening. Cat has made fun of me so many times for it that I've lost count. Like, two years ago when we were in a local summer production of *Legally Blonde The Musical* and I had a crush on the boy who played Emmett for basically the entire run but didn't say a thing. Cat got so frustrated, she literally pushed me in his direction during the cast party, thus forcing us into conversation. Except that when we started to talk, he was just . . . kind of boring? A boring personality can immediately eliminate a crush. Then there was this time I liked the Starbucks boy at the shop in town and told Cat that I thought he might be my soul mate only to totally lose interest the next week. She made fun of me for that one for months.

But this trip is not about me, so even if I am flirting with the person I met two seconds ago, I need to stop getting off track and focus on my goal. Which is to get Max nice and distracted and happy while we travel around Israel. Priorities and all that.

Max comes back with the last two people, who apparently had the audacity to go ahead and use the bathroom.

David has a list of all our names, which he double-checks. "Right, I guess I need to . . ." He gestures toward the group.

"You got this," I say.

He nods at me and then turns to face the group. "Hi, I'm—" he starts too quietly. He raises his voice. "Hey! Everyone! Okay, hi. I'm David Damari, the Madrich. We're going to get our bags, go through security, and meet up with the rest of the group. Onward!"

For a second, I wonder why there is so much security.

Except I guess it makes sense. We're in Israel.

I grew up thinking about this place in terms of my family. When I signed us up for this trip, my first priority was helping Max. But there was this other layer too. I was excited. This is where our grandma grew up. Maybe we'd feel closer to her, to that side of our family, if we actually visited where they were from.

My great-grandparents escaped the Holocaust by moving here. Most of their family members who stayed in Poland did not survive. Without this land, my family probably wouldn't be alive.

Israel is the only place in the world with a Jewish majority. Some believe this is important to give a voice in the global and political sphere to a whole group of people who have historically been persecuted. For some, it comes down to safety.

But the truth is, many people don't have such kind feelings toward Israel. And I get it.

Last year, I took a current events class for my history requirement. We had a whole unit on the Israeli-Palestinian conflict. I tried to imagine Safta and her family, where they were, what their lives looked like, as I read about the historical fights. When we got to modern day, though, it seemed so divorced from anything I heard my family talking about. I mean, as an American, it's not like I'm unfamiliar with a government making policies that are completely opposed to everything I believe in. Palestinians struggle to find basic necessities, health care, and job opportunities. I find many of the recent Israeli government policies toward them horrifying, and I imagine many Israelis feel the same way.

So while many Jews see this land as a safe harbor, many Palestinians feel about Israel like Native Americans feel about the US. Some of the problems are rooted in the British Mandate after WWI, when the UK government basically promised the same land to Jews, Arabs, and themselves. At the time, many Jews bought land in what then became Israel. So the land was legally sold, but it was also stolen. Since the foundation of Israel, millions of Palestinians have been displaced from their homes; many remain stuck in refugee camps with no rights and nowhere to go.

I remember talking to Safta when the Israeli government was in the news about the talks around annexing the West Bank. "Our family, we do not agree on this," Safta said over the phone. "No one supports it. We want peace; we all want peace. It is, the problem is, in Israel and in Palestine, we all do not agree on the terms."

So there's a hoard of political and geographic disputes, and at times of tension those disputes can turn into violence. The heightened security, I remind myself, is because of this. I wonder, though, if that security contributes to the atmosphere.

Will I have a better context for this conflict now that I'm actually here? Is this something we'll talk about? I know this is a temple trip, so we might not even get into politics. Maybe our focus will just be on tourist sites and religious study. I honestly don't know.

The other group leader (what did David call her? A Madricha?) is waiting for us outside security with a homemade sign, written in a neat script and bordered by adorable hand-drawn flowers. She's got on a loose sundress and strappy gladiator sandals. There's a scarf wrapped around her head like a headband. I think she's probably in her early twenties. She has some serious *artsy grandma who smokes nonmedical marijuana* vibes coming from her. I want her to teach me how to meditate.

She gathers us all with far more ease than either David or I was able to manage. "Hi, I'm Jess Goldstein. I'm the Madricha. I'm sure you all met David." She nods over in his direction. "He's the Madrich. Basically, that just means he's the boy staff member here and I'm the girl staff member. Our tour leader is going to meet us outside. There'll be a quick info sesh, some introductions, and then you'll have time to change if you want to. Hats and water bottles out!"

We mill into an open area outside, and it hits me. I'm Someplace Else. The first indicator is the sign, right above the exit, which is written in Arabic, Hebrew, and English. I have to assume that the English is there because English speakers as a whole don't take the time to invest in language education . . . or because of colonialism. One of those for sure.

The Hebrew letters curve like an artistic pattern I wish I could decipher. The most I can read in Hebrew are those letters on the dreidel, which is pretty embarrassing because I have family who literally speak and write this as their first language.

The second thing I notice is all the beige. The exterior of the airport, the walkway outside, and the pavement around the building are all tan, like an expert sandcastle builder designed them. The sun isn't helping the matter because it's so bright that everything seems slightly faded, like a photo capturing the light's glare. I'm going to need to invest in sunglasses while I'm here.

Then there's the weather. In comparison to a New

England winter, this place is *hot*. When I was packing, my weather app said it would be in the low sixties here this week, which hurts my head a little because two days ago, I was bundled up in a sweater opening Hanukkah and Christmas presents. Anything above freezing comes as a shock.

I leave my suitcase in this large pile we've formed at the edge of the walkway and head over to sit down next to Max. He found a spot in the very little shade available, thanks to a curved palm tree, and is already lounging like a typical man on public transportation. I push his leg a little so I, too, can partake in the *won't get pounded by the sun* portion of seating, a set of stone steps we have turned into an amphitheater. I notice that the steps don't really lead anywhere; they just end in tan stone that stretches out until it meets a parking lot. I wonder if they are purely decorative or strategically placed for group gatherings just like this.

I have to think that we have our whole group here already by how crowded these steps are. There are a couple of people searching for sunscreen in their suitcases, but otherwise we are all sitting down, waiting. Thank goodness Max snagged the shade.

Except I start to wonder if I should even be sitting next to him at all.

I look for Sammy. She's sitting a couple of steps ahead of us, directly in the sun.

"Max, Sammy's there," I say. "You should ask her to come sit with us."

"Why?" he asks.

"The shade," I say. "Plus, it'll be nice to have a friend on this trip who we haven't known since the womb."

Max shrugs, but then he says, "Hey, Sammy, we found some shade," and she walks over.

I talk a little at first because I did just claim I wanted a new friend, but then they start chatting about all the places they hope we'll go on the trip and the tentative itinerary our youth group sent us, and I just stop contributing. I can probably "accidentally" mention that she thinks he's cute by day two.

I wonder who I'll spend time with now that Max has Sammy. I look around at the group like someone might have a sign on them that says TALLY'S NEW FRIEND. If only things were that easy.

I hate making friends, largely because I'm out of practice. The last time I made a serious friend was at my elementary school picnic when I was five, an event hosted every summer to welcome new families and the incoming kindergarten class. Cat asked me if I wanted to play superhero detectives, and I said "duh." When it turned out she was in my class that year, we sat together. After a while, I realized I never wanted her to leave my side.

Not that I knew she was my person right away. She was just that overly active girl who came up with the best games during recess. I can't pinpoint when it shifted. Our first sleepover when we turned six? Third grade, when we were in different classes but still made a point to have weekly play-dates? Fifth grade, when she invited me on her family road trip to Maine? In my head, our friendship has always been a fact. Cat and Tally, Tally and Cat—like latkes and applesauce or mac and cheese.

I think about that beginning sometimes. The memory is muddled, just flashes of her red dress as we ran around the patchy field behind the school, the sound of overlapping giggles, the sweet taste of her lychees paired with my strawberries. I think about that as the moment that changed my life.

I wonder if any of the people on this trip will change my life too.

My eyes find David. He's standing on the makeshift stage, looking particularly giraffe-like next to tiny hippie Jess.

Another person walks over, a woman who probably isn't that much older than Jess but is definitely the Designated Adult here. She's got coarse reddish-brown hair and a stocky build, like she can and will fight someone. Jess gives her a warm hug; David offers a stiff handshake.

The grown-up person walks in front of the group. She claps her hands together a few times until everyone falls silent.

"Shalom, my name is Chaya; I'm your tour leader." Her accent sounds a lot like Safta's, vaguely French but just different enough to confuse strangers. "Welcome to Israel, bruchim habaim."

I know she just said something in Hebrew, but the meaning is lost on me. I think it was a blessing?

"About me," she continues. "My background is history; I

lead many tours in Israel. I even lead tours with your Jess before. We learn much here, we have fun, we experience. I will take you to fascinating sites full of history; we will visit the social and cultural life here. I'll give you the schedule tonight.

"Now, I need to say some things. You stick with the group. We are in the desert. Your head, always covered when outside. Baseball hat, scarf, I don't care. You cover, you put on sunscreen, you drink water. You drink and drink and drink."

Jess walks forward next to Chaya. "Guys, I know we sound pushy with this, but it's really serious. We just want you to have fun, enjoy the whole experience. So don't be idiots. Cover the top of your head, refill your water bottle. We'll keep reminding you too." She smiles, pats Chaya's arm, and takes a step back.

"Yes, I will give you many reminders. Now, I have something else: drinking alcohol. I know a lot of you will think that you can party if you are eighteen. No, you are in high school. Your bodies are not used to alcohol; you are jet-lagged. Don't be foolish." Some people start whispering at this, but it doesn't really affect me. I don't drink; it's a whole thing with my anxiety. I like having control too much. Plus, I've seen how dangerous drinking can be.

Jess steps forward again. "Just one more thing, I swear, and then you can get out of those airplane clothes." She reaches into her bag and pulls out a banner. It's nothing like the cute little sign she had for us when we arrived. It's hard-core and official-looking, plastic with big typed lettering that reads: #IVEGOTCHUTZPAH. "Temple Beth El had this made up for our trip. I'm sure you will all be taking lots of pictures. If there's a really cool shot and you want to grab the banner, we will always have it with us. And make sure to tag our youth group!

"We'll bug you all more later, don't worry," Jess adds. "For now, go change. Bathrooms are inside, to the right. The bus is out those doors on the left. Everyone needs to be accounted for and ready to get out of here in twenty minutes. Go!"

We all sluggishly grab our bags and head to freshen up. I'm more than ready to get out of my leggings and sweatshirt. They were nice and cozy for the flight, but now they're feeling a little itchy and I think they smell? I might be overthinking.

There's already a line when I get to the bathroom. I unzip the top of my suitcase to see if I have anything relatively cute near the top. There's an oversize shirt, which is now wrinkled, and a striped dress . . . which is also pretty wrinkled at this point.

I'm busy rummaging through the top of my bag when a girl ahead of me in line says, "Hey, you."

I look up. "Um, yes?"

The girl who is talking to me looks too cool to be talking to me. She has a shaved head and perfectly full eyebrows. Even her airplane outfit looks trendy, wide-legged pants and a crop top.

"I propose an exchange of sorts," she says. "You watch

my suitcase while I'm changing, and I watch yours when it's your turn."

"Sure," I say. "You're on the Temple Beth El trip too, right?" I ask.

"Yeah! I basically freaked out when I found out they were offering a high school exchange trip; I've always wanted to come here. I'm actually from a different congregation; my family goes to Beth Shalom. I'm Saron Melaku, by the way," she adds. "Sah-ron," she repeats slowly, like she's used to people getting it wrong. She isn't wearing her name tag, so I'm glad for the intro.

"Tally Gelmont," I say.

"Like tally marks?" she asks.

"Like short for Talia," I say.

"I like you, Tally Mark," she says. "I can just tell with people."

She keeps talking as we wait for our turn to change. She tells me about her family, who moved from Ethiopia to Framingham right before she was born. By the time she heads into the stall to put on the red romper she's been holding in her hands, I know she's the oldest of four, a high school senior like me, and speaks four languages: Amharic, English, Hebrew, and French.

"You're up, Tally Mark," Saron says. She added statement lips and sunglasses while she was in the stall. She looks like a model who is trying unsuccessfully to hide from the paparazzi.

I decide to try on the wrinkled top, leggings, and Converse. I think I look somewhat decent until I open the door and Saron shakes her head.

"What are the other options?" she asks.

I look down. "Oh no, is it that wrinkled?"

"It's fine, Tally Mark. Perfectly ordinary. But this is our first day in Israel. You need to wear something extraordinary."

"I have other clothes," I say.

At this point, she's now opened up my suitcase and is looking through my clothes. "That," she says, pulling out an off-the-shoulder black dress.

"That's more of a night thing," I say.

She nods. "You're completely right. Oh, this," she says, holding out a pale-green sweater dress. "I have the perfect necklace to go with it."

"Okay," I say. "Are you sure?"

"Definitely," she says.

I go back and change. The dress feels a little short without leggings or jeans underneath.

"Yes," Saron says when I walk out. "Here, I'll help you put this on," she adds, holding up the necklace, a black choker that looks like she went back in time and stole it from the nineties.

I look in the mirror. I still seem a little tired, and my mousy brown hair is up in its permanent high ponytail, all curly at the ends, but I guess the whole look *is* cute. The dress makes my hazel eyes look more green than brown, and the choker makes it seem like this is a purposeful look.

"Just a little highlighter and some dark lips and you're set," Saron says.

"Oh, I don't think—" I start.

"You're totally right," she says. "All natural. What a

statement." She pulls up the handle on her suitcase. "See you on the bus, Tally Mark."

I look back at myself. I know how to do a little stage makeup, but most of the times when I've needed normal makeup, Cat has helped me out. She became obsessed with makeup tutorials when we were in middle school, meaning, of course, that I became her doll.

But Cat isn't here. I'm on my own. I put on some lip balm and add a little foundation under my eyes so I don't look like I haven't slept, then head to the bus.

WHERE DO YOU BELONG?

I'm sitting next to Max, trying to get more sleep, but some demonic soul has decided to blast annoyingly loud, vaguely Middle Eastern–sounding music through the bus. There are a few people singing along, super excited as the speakers boom about being a golden boy and showing people Tel Aviv. I slip out my headphones and silently thank the tech gods for the invention of portable chargers because I've been relying on my phone, which is now firmly placed in airplane mode for the remainder of the trip, for music. I offer Max an earbud, but he shakes his head.

I stare at the back of the chair in front of me, willing myself to feel sleepy. Maybe if I focus on the blue upholstery, I will get so bored that I will just conk out. The glare from the window is too bright, though, and the music on the bus is so loud that I can hear it over the soothing piano music I'm listening to on my headphones.

My eyes wander to David.

He's at the front of the bus having what looks like a Serious Talk with Chaya and Jess and our armed security guard, Batya, because that's a thing we apparently have on the trip. I think this might be the first time they've met in person, and now they're in charge of herding thirty young adults, aged sixteen to eighteen, through Israel. Good luck to them.

I'm trying to decide whether David is good-looking or not. Like objectively, sure, if tall guys are your thing. And his arms look . . . nice. I can see them now through his Georgetown T-shirt. But I don't know. What does it even mean to be attractive? I can look at someone and be like, all right, sure, you fit my westernized views of beauty, but does that even mean anything? Are you kind? Are you silly? Which makes me think about this quote from *Doctor Who* where Amy Pond is talking about Rory, the love of her life, and she says that sometimes after you get to know a person, their personality is sort of written all over their face and that is beautiful.

I've never been in love like Amy Pond.

In no time, we're in Jaffa. The ride couldn't have been more than a half hour. I didn't even get in a power nap.

Once we're outside, I can feel the sun already kicking my butt, so I take out some sunscreen. I missed this last week when I was dealing with winter in Massachusetts. The thing is, my Irish/Ashkenazi combo skin has given me a vampiric attitude toward the sun. Look, I respect it, but a girl has got to be prepared or she'll burst into a pile of dust and/or get a sunburn.

Chaya leads us to another set of steps.

"Hats and water bottles!" Jess chimes before walking to sit down with us. I have my dad's old Red Sox cap in my bag, but I'm attempting to hold out until absolutely necessary because it will definitely ruin my look. My *Hamilton* water bottle is in my bag too, but it's almost empty.

Chaya claps her hands to get our attention. "Welcome to Israel!" she says. "This is the Jaffa Port. It's a beautiful port, eh? It's a beautiful city. I have a story of the port and then we talk about the trip. We talk about what it means to be here. We talk of the map. So yes, let's start!"

I absentmindedly look around at the group. I've got to be one of the older people here, which is a weird feeling. I mean, I *am* a senior. According to basically every TV show/movie, that is supposed to mean something. I should be wise, a role model, possibly married with a baby and a successful rock tour under my belt.

David said he's a college freshman. I wonder how old Chaya is—somewhere around thirty? What about Batya, in charge of holding a gun and protecting us? I honestly have no concept of how old she could be.

Or Sammy, for that matter. Maybe she's secretly really young, and the age difference between her and Max would weird her out. I wonder if she's said anything about her age. I should've pulled a Mr. Beard El Al employee and asked her.

I'm spiraling. In the past, when I've started to panic, Cat's been there to help me. When I began having panic attacks, she did all this research on breathing techniques and meditation. What am I supposed to do without someone reminding me to breathe?

Chaya is telling a story about the founding of the Jaffa Port, and I'm sure it would be more meaningful if I were properly awake and not worried about my plan. Plus, she assured us we have a full day of programming. Full. Day. After getting off an airplane. An airplane we were on for More Than Ten Hours. That just seems mean.

Maybe that'll be good for Max, though. He'll be so busy, he won't have any time to feel sad.

Once we're finished with Chaya's lecture, I'm *ready* to eat. She leads us back near where we got off the bus and tells us we have an hour and a half to eat and explore the local shuk, which apparently means "market." "I'm going to get shakshuka—eggs and tomato. I also recommend the pastries here." She points. "There is joint, eh, how do you say—it's the Arabs and Jews working together."

Which leads us to the awkward part: forming groups. Most of us are strangers, with the occasional pair of siblings or cousins or friends thrown in. I'm glad I have Max here. That is, until I see him standing next to Sammy.

"You coming?" Max asks.

"No," I say. "If we start out all attached at the hip, we're not going to make any new friends. We'll just be those freakishly close loner twins."

Max gives me a look like he already thinks I'm being freakish. "Sure, Tal," he says. He turns to Sammy, pointing to the bakery Chaya recommended.

Which leaves me standing by myself. Not ideal, but I can probably figure something out. I look for my new fashion friend, Saron, but she must have already left for food.

So I'm alone. Great. Fine. I'll probably just get lost and then separated from the group and then die in an Israeli alleyway.

I feel a tap on my shoulder.

"You hungry?" David asks. I didn't even notice him walk over.

I nod.

"There's this falafel place I went to last time I was here. Do you like falafel?" David asks.

"I've been known to enjoy it from time to time."

He smiles, and it's a cute smile. Objectively. Through my westernized lens of beauty.

"We can cut through the shuk," he says, waving us forward. The shuk turns out to be a set of what almost looks like alleyways that have been draped in jewelry and fabrics and assorted works of art, like a big flea market plopped between ancient buildings. There's a big tented area, too, with tables covered in hats and scarves and other random products for purchase. About half have Stars of David on them.

The market is quiet for all its clutter. There are a few other people walking around, examining goods, but for the most part, we hear only vendors, making the occasional remark on their wares.

"Taglit?" one of the sellers calls out to us. "Ah, Taglit, yeah?"

I raise my eyebrow. *Tag-leet?*

"What'd he call me?" I ask David, voice low.

"It was really nasty, doesn't translate," David says. Then he smirks. "No, no, he said Taglit. It's what they call Birthright over here; he must think we're on one of their trips. The word means 'discovery.'"

"Ah, a trip of discovery. I always heard it was about hooking up and drinking and propaganda."

I had a couple of friends from drama club who went on Birthright after they graduated. When they talked about it, it was mostly centered on jokes about hooking up with Israeli soldiers, partying, and coupling off to continue the Jewish line.

I mean, they talked about other stuff too. One of them said that she felt more connected to her family after the trip. I guess I don't really know how I feel about it.

David laughs. "That and nothing else," he says. "I actually had a really great time on my Birthright trip." His voice is more serious now. "I mean, they do go hard on the Jewish perspective of things—it *is* partly funded by the Israeli government—but I was pretty lucky with my tour guide. Talked openly about the Israeli-Palestinian conflict, checkpoints, border disputes, occupations. Granted, we didn't hear from any Palestinians." David pauses. "I have friends who went on other trips, and it was a totally different experience. I think it changes a lot group to group."

"Why did they name it Birthright, though?" I continue. "I know the history is complicated, but the implications there are . . . not great."

"Honestly, I feel like the Hebrew name is more representative. Of my experience, at least," David says. "'Discovery.'

"You know, I think we can make this a trip of discovery too," he adds.

"Yeah? What exactly am I supposed to discover on this trip?"

"A deep connection to Judaism, obviously," David says.

"Obviously," I repeat. "I expect to be seventy-five percent more Jewish by the end of the trip."

"The temple wouldn't be doing its job otherwise. Personally, I'm aiming for eighty-five percent."

I laugh.

We make it to the falafel place. It's small, with a counter laid out like a sandwich shop occupying most of the space. We order, picking through what to add, falafel, hummus, tomatoes, and even fries, before finding two seats at a table that barely fits our plates.

The food is delicious; David was right. I basically swallow mine whole because my table manners are just that good. He's still eating.

"So, Georgetown," I say.

"Yeah, how did you—right, the shirt." He looks down. "Political Science. You?"

"Boston University," I say, which is technically true. I got in early decision. But then I add, "Next year. I'm a senior."

"Right, of course you're in high school." He shakes his head. "So much ahead in your life. Take it from a wizened old person like myself."

"Psh, I already feel old. I'm graduating in June."

"I'm sure your bones have gone brittle."

"Oh, my back," I say, playing along.

"Sometimes it feels like it's been ages since I was in high school," he continues. "Then other days, I wake up and I'm like, 'Oh no! Ms. Kazinsky is giving us a test, and I suddenly have no access to my clothes.'"

"Ms. Kazinsky?" I ask.

"Junior year physics teacher." He shudders.

"Oh, I'm great at physics! I'll help you study as soon as you find those clothes," I offer.

He laughs. "Good to know I've got a willing tutor."

I can see his phone, sitting on the table in front of him, light up with a message. He curses under his breath. "I'm so sorry—Jess is looking for me." He points to the screen. Must have international coverage. "Duty calls." He stands up and then realizes he is about to leave me alone in a foreign place. "Are you here with anyone?"

"My brother, Max. He went to the bakery."

"Perfect. I'll drop you off over there and then get to work. Us old people have to make a living somehow."

We walk to the bakery, following the twists and turns of the shuk. I'm awful with directions, but I think David is mostly retracing our steps because I recognize some of the stalls we passed earlier. We even go by the "Taglit" vendor. David is a few paces ahead of me, but he keeps looking back, to make sure I'm still with him. I feel like this is why people hold hands in a public place: to make sure they don't lose each other.

Not that I'm thinking about holding David's hand. Because that would be way too soon, and honestly I've never held a guy's hand before and, like, slow down; this is a stranger, and—

I rub the bead on my fidget ring, the bumpy surface soothing against my finger.

The bakery is just down the road from our meeting point, and Max is thankfully still there. I can see him sitting outside on the curb with a few other people from our group, a pastry in his hand. Behind them are glass displays stacked high with different kinds of baked goods I can't identify, rounded blue stones decorating the exterior. I start to walk over.

David waves goodbye and then salutes, too, for some reason? Dork.

"You're back," Max says.

I sit down on the sidewalk next to him. My dress is so short that I have to awkwardly angle my legs so that I'm not showing off my underwear and, even then, part of my bare leg is on the ground, the stones a little rough against my skin.

I'm surprised that it isn't just Max and Sammy; I would have eaten with them if I'd known they would be with a group.

I end up talking to Sammy. She seems nice; she only turned eighteen a week ago, so that's one fear down, now that I know she is practically the same age as us and isn't a really old-looking thirteen-year-old who secretly scammed her way onto a trip for Jewish high schoolers.

"Have you applied to any schools yet?" I ask, keeping my voice light and conversational.

"Oh, a ton! I sent in fourteen applications. Last week.

I was going to hold myself back because it's so expensive, but getting into schools can be competitive and my parents paid for half and I've been working at our JCC, so it seemed like the right choice."

She works at a Jewish Community Center? I don't even know if we have a JCC in our town. I think about bringing up my Israeli grandma, like it might prove that I deserve to be here.

I mean, of course I deserve to be here. We're all Jewish. Even if some of us have never stepped foot in a JCC.

"Any in Boston?" I ask. "I'm going to BU. Early decision," I explain. "Our mom teaches there, religious studies."

"Oh, that's really cool," she says, voice genuine. "I'm so jealous of people who already know where they're going," she adds. "One of my best friends got in early to Emerson, and I think I physically turned green when she told me." She lets out a little puff of breath, like she's amused herself with her own joke.

I can't stand when people say things like *one of my best friends*. How can you have more than one *best* friend? There's only one who can be the best.

Maybe I should feel bad for her. Not everyone is lucky enough to have a true best friend.

"Sorry, you asked if I applied to schools in Boston, and I go off and tell you about someone else. I applied to Northeastern," she finally says.

Perfect. BU and Northeastern are practically in the same part of the city.

I'm waiting for this to turn to Max; he hasn't really said anything since I sat down. Maybe this will inspire him to say that he's going to apply to schools in Boston too. Instead, he wraps up the wax paper that was holding his pastry and gets up to throw it in the trash.

Cool cool cool. At least I tried.

When we're done, we meet up with the group for a quick bathroom stop and then head onto the bus.

I sit back down next to Max. I wonder if I should find a new seat buddy so he has to interact with other people. I look around the bus. My bathroom-clothing-consultant friend, Saron, is at the very back. She has her stuff spread out on the seat next to her and a sketch pad balanced on her lap. She's one of the only people sitting alone.

"Now you rest," Chaya says. "We have hours here on the bus, then the hostel." She sits down. Thankfully, no one turns on any music.

I turn my own music back on, and this time I'm actually able to fall asleep.

SO FAR AWAY

The first place we're staying is a hostel way up in the northern region of Israel. I thought hostels were supposed to be sort of trashy, but this place seems decent. There's a big dining area that looks like a school cafeteria off the lobby, and the rooms are pretty bare, just beds with stiff white sheets and a bathroom. At least it's clean, so I don't have to worry about sleeping here.

Sammy and I are assigned as roommates, which feels quite serendipitous. The universe obviously arranged this.

She decided to take a quick shower before dinner, so I'm basically alone in the room. I sit down on the edge of the bed.

I should take a power nap . . . or a power nap extension. That rest time on the bus did not make up for my lack of sufficient airplane sleep. My whole body feels heavy, like someone piled weights on top of me. I get as far as lying down, still in the green dress I wore all day, when I remember that Mom made me promise to call as soon as Max and I were settled.

I connect to the Wi-Fi and FaceTime her.

"You remembered me!" she says as a greeting.

"Who?" I ask. "Sorry, random stranger, this is a butt dial."

She ignores me. "How was the flight?"

"Short and breezy. We arrived in three seconds flat."

"Good, good," she says. "Moshe, the kids are on the phone. They invented spontaneous transportation."

"Kid," I correct.

"The girl is on the phone," Mom calls out.

"Oh, good. We like that one better, right?" I can hear Dad ask from off-screen.

"At the moment, she's the only one who called," Mom answers.

I can see Dad's chin and torso. He's wearing this obnoxious Hanukkah sweater that Max gave him, even though Hanukkah is over. "*Bubbeleh!*" he says.

"*Mamale sheli,*" I finish.

Technically, I just called my dad a "little mother." It's become this thing that we say to each other, mostly because of Safta. Whenever we talk to her, she throws as many Yiddish terms of endearment at us as possible and liberally adds the diminutive -*le* to the ends of our names.

"You survived your flight," he says, sitting down on the couch next to my mom so I can see his face on the camera.

"Barely. I didn't really sleep."

"Tally," Mom says, voice serious. "You need to make sure you're taking care of yourself."

"I am," I say.

"You know we worry," Mom says. "Ever since the accident . . ."

"It's not like I was the one in the car," I say quickly.

Mom glances at Dad in this unspoken exchange of concern. I hate when they do this sort of thing. I'm not the child they should be worried about.

"How's it been?" Dad asks, breaking the tension.

"We saw Jaffa," I say.

"The port," Dad says. "Isn't it beautiful?"

I nod.

"Have you been to the Western Wall yet?" Mom asks. "Oh, Tally, you'll just love it. Did you know that it was originally a part of the Temple Mount, and it's actually the remaining structure from—"

"The second temple, most of which was destroyed by the Romans," I finish. I've heard this lecture at least four times. "And no, just Jaffa today."

"Well, you'll love it when you go. I swear, you'll feel spiritually whole there."

For a professor, my mom sure loves her spirituality. You'd think teaching would make her more focused on logic and reason, but here we are.

"We have dinner soon and then some meeting debrief thing before bed, but I just wanted to let you know we're both okay."

"She's already trying to get us off the phone," Mom says to Dad.

"We're boring compared to Israel," he responds.

"You two are the worst," I cut in. They both look back at me.

"We love you too," Mom says.

"Send pictures," Dad adds.

I say goodbye and hang up.

It's weird being away from Mom and Dad. I guess I'll have to get used to that next year when I go to college. BU is only a half hour from home, though, and it's not like I'll be alone. Mom comes into the city four days a week for class, and Max will be there too.

When Cat found out our plan to apply to BU, she promptly decided she would go to Boston College.

"We'll be rivals, then; it'll spice up our friendship."

"Do they even have a theater program?" I asked at the time.

"Like my dad would ever let me go to an arts program," she said. I thought Cat could convince Mr. Yang to let her do just about anything, but I didn't fight her on it. Especially after she added, "I can't leave you."

That was that. Cat decided she would go to BC to study business, with the secret intention of opening her own theater company, and Max and I would go to BU. We agreed that we'd all get an apartment together in Brookline for our last two years of college.

I'm still holding my phone, wasting time. I open up Instagram, pondering whether I should post any pictures from today, but end up scrolling through my feed aimlessly instead.

That's when I see her.

There's a picture of Cat, bowing onstage. She's wearing

her Miss Hannigan costume: a dress, cardigan, and chunky, oversize necklace. We actually bought the cardigan together because Cat wasn't satisfied with the options in the costume closet. We made a whole shopping day out of it.

She was always more into the productions as a whole— the clothes, the lighting, the staging. For me, everything paled in comparison to the songs. Before the whole writer's block business, at least.

Which is why Cat decided on what she deemed the perfect solution to combat my inability to write new lyrics: the silent treatment.

"This is for your own good," she said, lying across the end of my bed. "It'll give you the motivation to focus. If you can't hang out with your favorite person, me, then you'll have to write even faster."

"That's not how inspiration works," I groaned, propped up against a stack of pillows. But for some reason, I agreed.

This is for your own good, I think now, putting down my phone.

I'm so used to doing everything together. What am I supposed to do without her here?

$$\Longrightarrow \text{------} \Longleftarrow$$

I take a quick shower after Sammy does; then we head to dinner.

"I assume they'll have kosher options?" she asks, voice worried.

She keeps kosher? My family has never followed any dietary restrictions, especially not religious ones.

"They have to," I say. "You let them know you keep kosher, right?" That was one of those standard questions the trip organizers asked before we came here, like whether we have allergies or any health conditions they should know about before they send us off on a plane.

She nods. "I know. I just get convinced there won't be anything real. Not like it's usually a problem in Israel . . ."

Sammy doesn't have to worry. There's hummus and fresh cucumber and bright red tomatoes and pita. There's also something that I think might be fish, but even I'm not touching it. I wonder if I'm going to have to survive mostly on hummus on this trip.

Max is already sitting at one of the long tables. I feel like we are about to have lunch at school. All that's missing is for Cat to drop her tray of food on the table across from us and launch into an unprompted story.

I sit across from Max; Sammy sits next to him. We're eating pretty quietly, speculating a little about what this meeting will be about tonight, when Saron sits down next to me.

"Tally Mark! I thought I'd dreamed you up in a post-plane haze." She looks at Sammy and Max. "You found other friends already; you're fast."

Max raises an eyebrow. *Tally Mark?* he mouths.

I shrug.

"This is my brother, Max," I say, pointing across the table. "This is Sammy. We're roommates for the night."

"Saron," she says, pointing to herself. She says it slowly again. "You changed," she adds, looking directly at me.

"Oh, the necklace is in my room; I can—"

"No," she says. "You might need it later. Plus, I've decided that we're friends, Tally Mark."

"Thanks?"

"So," Saron continues. "What are we going to get up to tonight? I'm ready for some unsanctioned, after-hours bonding."

"That could be fun," Sammy says, voice excited.

"Oh, I don't know," Max says. "I was thinking about sleeping as soon as our group meeting is over."

He's trying to sleep instead of spend time with people? This is a bad sign. This is a depressive sign. This is an *I'll never apply to college because I don't care about anything* sign. So I say the one thing that I know will guarantee he socializes tonight. "We could play Cards Against Humanity."

Games are a Thing in our family. A sometimes competitive Thing, sure, but a Thing all the same.

"Oh, well, if we're going to play Cards Against Humanity, then I have to be in," he says.

He's so lucky he has me.

TONIGHT

I packed the cards in my suitcase, so after a debrief with our whole group, I'm tasked with retrieving the game. As I'm leaving the room, I accidentally walk right into David, smacking him with the card box.

"Are you okay?" I ask quickly, a weird adrenaline running through my veins. "I had no idea . . . I didn't mean . . . I was just rushing and . . . Are you hurt?"

He rubs his side. "I got a little closer to that box than I expected to, but I'm fine," he says. "Is that Cards Against Humanity?

"I love Cards Against Humanity," he adds before I can answer. "I have this magic ability where I just know what someone else will think is funny. As long as my cards aren't duds, I always win."

"And as long as the moon isn't out, it's always daytime," I say.

"Hey!" he says. "It's a real skill."

"Sure, but I really can't believe you until I see it."

Which is how David ends up joining our group.

"'Licking things to claim them as your own,' 'panda sex,' 'classist undertones,' 'dick fingers,' 'a mopey zoo lion,' and 'lumberjack fantasies,'" he reads, looking at the cards in front of him. "Guys, I'm a little worried about your views on my relationship status."

"I knew I should have just played 'masturbation,'" Max says with a sigh.

Gross.

It's past midnight now, and we are deep into our game. We're sitting outside on a grassy outlook between the hostel bedrooms and the entrance, bundled up so we can play under the stars. The competition is heated. Max threatened to beat us all so completely that we'd be embarrassed for the rest of the trip, said with the bravado of his former game-loving self. It clearly is not working, though, because David and I are tied for the lead.

I'm not sure about any magic abilities or special skills, but he's pretty good.

"I'm going to go with 'licking things to claim them as your own.'"

"Thank you very much," I say, holding out my hand for the black card.

"Who told you about my licking habit?" he asks, his voice full of mock offense.

"No one. Just a vibe you give off."

"Licking anyone in particular now?" asks Saron.

Wow, I think I just willed her to ask that with my mind so I wouldn't have to.

"Oh, I haven't licked anyone in a while," he says and then immediately blushes.

"I like licking multiple people at the same time," Saron says.

"Licking can be fun," Max adds.

"Can we please stop talking about licking?" I ask. Now my face is nice and red. I pick at a piece of grass, tearing it into tiny pieces as a distraction.

"You're the one who played the card," Max points out.

"You're my brother. I don't want to think about you . . . licking people."

"Yet you're fine thinking about David licking people," Max says, and honestly, I'm going to smack him so hard the moment we are alone. Maybe stab him? Maiming is completely justified when your brother is being a jerk.

"I played a winning card; you're just jealous. Actually, I'm at seven now, so . . ."

"How dare you, David! You let her win," Max says.

"It's not my fault your sister is funny."

"And you're not," I add.

I zip up the top of my new BU fleece. There's a chill in the night air that's cold enough to make me think that we really should be inside. Since we're in the northern region of the country, we can actually see other countries off in the distance. We're going to be here for a couple of nights before heading back to Tel Aviv to actually spend some time in the city. Chaya handed out a tentative schedule at our meeting, which will apparently be a nightly routine so we can prepare for the day ahead and debrief. Tonight's theme was about hopes and expectations for the trip, capped off with some scheduling. We need to be at breakfast around seven AM tomorrow, which I'm already dreading.

Every single day is packed with activities, and I'm realizing I wasn't 100 percent sure what I was signing us up for on this trip. Like, tomorrow we are hiking and rafting and going to a winery? Then there's a museum and historical sights and long bus rides that will basically take us all over the country.

"Okay, I'm calling it a night," Saron says, standing up. She dusts off the strands of grass that are sticking to her legs. "I'll see you all way too early tomorrow," she says as a good night, already walking away.

I start to get up too. "Heading back to the room, Sammy?" I ask.

"I'm going to stay out here a little bit longer," she says.

Max hasn't said he's going back to his room yet, meaning there's the strong potential that they will be talking under the stars. How absurdly romantic.

"I'll leave the door unlocked for you." I turn to head for my room, holding my smile until my back is turned toward them.

"I'll walk with you," David offers. "I've heard dark and scary things lurk around here."

"What a mensch. Glad I have you to protect me," I say. We turn the corner to the section with the dorms.

"Psh, you've got to protect me," he says.

"I did take a self-defense class last year . . . Eyes! Groin!" I mock poke out an invisible enemy's eyes and knee him in his imaginary privates.

"I feel so much safer," David says.

We're at my door, since it was basically around the corner. "This is me," I say.

"Right, of course," he says. "Don't attack anyone else tonight, unless they deserve it." Then he adds with a smile, "Good night." He does his silly little salute goodbye.

Ugh, why do I find that endearing? Why do I always do this? Seriously, it's like the first time someone even talks to me and I have a fully formed crush and hopes and dreams. There's no way this can work out. We're on a ten-day trip, and he's a staff member and older than I am.

And and and.

For a second, I do give it some weight. It wouldn't be the worst thing . . .

I picture all the activities Chaya told us about at the meeting: rafting and hiking and a museum trip. I can see myself sitting on a raft as the water rushes by, laughing, or walking past a row of paintings, scribbling notes in my journal. David's there, next to me as I raft and hike and wander around a museum. Imaginary me seems so completely in the moment and so completely happy.

I shake my head. I shouldn't think like that. I need to focus on Max.

I go to bed with a guilty feeling, like acid in the back of my throat . . . though thoughts of David are still at the front of my mind.

GO THE DISTANCE

Now that I'm no longer basically an extra in a low-budget zombie movie thanks to some sleep, I'm ready to focus on my true trip goal: getting Max back to normal. Today is the day. Now that I've rested, I can do anything.

My plan is deceptively simple. I'm going to spend the day making sure he socializes, which is pretty much a guarantee thanks to our group. Withdrawing from social interactions is another sign of depression, which I know because Google told me. Therefore, socializing has to help. I'll liberally pepper in questions about college so that by the time he's feeling normal, he'll be primed and ready to apply.

All of this will culminate in my big move tonight when I accidentally let it slip that Sammy thinks he's cute. I'll have to get him alone, probably just by saying we should call Mom and Dad. I remember how awful he was showing off for Alyssa Greenburg. There's no way this can go wrong.

There's a breakfast buffet, cafeteria-style. I pile on my plate some of that shakshuka dish Chaya told us about earlier before adding a hearty scoop of hummus and a pita and making myself a cup of coffee.

As I'm balancing my plate and trying not to spill coffee everywhere as I walk to the tables, Saron spots me. She calls out, "Sit with me, Tally Mark," and pats the spot next to her.

I see Max, already eating at another table. He's not alone; he's sitting with some other guys from the group. My plan is already working, and I didn't even have to do anything.

"It really is just Tally," I say as I put down my food.

She shakes her head. "You can't change the nickname someone gives you. My little sister called me Sasa when she was learning to talk, and I'm stuck with it now."

"Does that mean I should call you Sasa?" I ask.

"No," she says definitively. "It means that we can't control other people. Personally, I'm quite uncontrollable."

I see Sammy walk over, a plate of food in her hands. I think she's going to sit with Max, but then she turns toward our table.

"Hey, morning!" she says, taking a seat. "Oh, there's coffee," she adds, eyeing my cup. "How did I miss that?"

"Over there." Saron points.

"Thanks," Sammy says. "I didn't get much sleep last night."

I vaguely remember her coming back into the room, but I had already gone to sleep, so the memory is fuzzy and dreamlike. I have no concept of what time it was when she went to bed.

"What exactly *were* you up to?" Saron asks, voice suggestive. "You were with Max, right?"

I bite my lip. Is this confirmation that they stayed up last night talking?

"Oh, we both went to bed soon after you all bowed out. I just have a hard time with jet lag; my internal clock is off."

I look over at Max, sitting at the other table. He isn't talking to anyone, just quietly eating his food.

It's fine, I remind myself. I have a plan. And I shouldn't expect him to just fix himself after one day in Israel.

After breakfast, I gather my stuff for the day's activities: sunscreen, water bottle, hat, and all the things for rafting now neatly packed in my day bag. I head to the bus.

"Want to sit in the back?" Max asks as we board.

Clearly he needs a little nudge in the right direction. "No, you should sit with someone else," I say. "Making friends, remember?"

He shakes his head a little and walks farther into the bus. Sammy is sitting alone, but he sits down behind two of the boys he had breakfast with instead.

I could go sit with her, I guess, but then I spot Saron. There's a seat open next to her.

She doesn't say anything for a full minute after I sit down. She has out a sketch pad, balanced on her lap. She's intently drawing in beiges and browns what looks like a ball gown. The model she's drawn is rough, all sharp lines, but the dress is detailed and precise so that the two look like they don't belong on the same page. I realize that she's working on a pattern of mountains within the frame of the dress.

"Is that for a school project?" I ask.

She shakes her head without stopping her work. "Application portfolio. I got it into my head that I'd find inspiration for my final piece on this trip," she explains. "It's a political commentary. I'm going to juxtapose the silhouette with the design on the fabric, essentially taking something that's elite and pairing it with the Syrian mountainscape, so beautiful itself despite the recent turmoil. If I actually make this, I'll hand paint the mountains." She pauses, looking at her drawing. "Maybe I'll dip the bottom in red dye and add some beadwork to look like shrapnel to call out the generalized horrifying ambivalence around ongoing violence . . . or is that too obvious?"

I genuinely don't know how to respond to that. Though I apparently don't need to, because Saron takes out a maroon pencil from the thin tin case in her purse and adds brushes of red unevenly along the hem of her two-dimensional ball gown.

She draws for the entirety of the ride.

"Hats and water bottles!" Jess says once the bus stops. I'm already wearing the Red Sox cap.

The hike is not a full-fledged hike, thank goodness. A Hike Lite, if you will. It reminds me of this reserve a couple of towns over that Girls Scouts use for camping. I'm sure the vegetation is different, but I really can't tell the difference, with the exception of the ground, which seems lighter than the deep browns of the dirt back home.

We stop at a set of logs, arranged like a small classroom. I wonder how many different groups have sat here and listened to a lecture on Israel.

"I want to share something," Chaya starts. "This is, eh, not what all tour leaders will say. When I think of my Jewishness, I have to think of the other part. There is more to me than just as a Jew.

"I did not grow up Orthodox in a traditional way, yet living in Israel, many things are Orthodox. The food we eat, Shabbat. Even most schools, though some are more Orthodox than others.

"I want to share something personal. If I get married, my partner will be a woman. I could not get married here, not like other people. There are religious reasons for that . . . religious reasons that do not fit with how I see Judaism.

"I'm sure many of you think that this trip has an agenda. It is organized by your temples. Well, I have an agenda too. I want us to speak and think about what it means to us to be a Jew.

"That is what we will be talking about. And we will have many, many opinions. I will have stories of the history for you as well, but I hope that what we take from the talks is meaning. That we think, how am I a Jew? What is a Jew? What can we do better?"

Chaya waves at us to get up and start walking again.

Saron turns to me. "I'm in love. She's too old for me, but I'm in love. I bet there's someone we can set her up with."

I laugh. "I think that's against the rules."

"Of course you're one of those. A rule follower." She shakes her head.

We continue the hike until we reach a waterfall. There's

a man-made deck and railing, constructed to have a perfect view of the water, crashing white over a small cliff of rocks that are framed by hanging leaves. The water collects into a pool of teal, crisp in the light, then flows into a stream, rushing over slick brown rocks.

Everyone takes absurd amounts of pictures. I notice two boys take a picture with the banner. One of them has it draped around his head as his "hat," while he lovingly cradles his water bottle as his friend calls out instructions like they're in the midst of a professional photo shoot.

As we're walking back, I feel a tap on my shoulder.

"Why are you being such a weirdo?" Max whispers.

"What?" I ask, turning around.

"A. Weirdo," he repeats. "You wouldn't sit with me for breakfast or on the bus. You refused to get lunch with me yesterday."

"I'm not being a weirdo; you're the weirdo." We were already near the back of the group, but now people are starting to pass us. Which means that we are going to be left behind calling each other weird back and forth forever until we die of dehydration.

"No, you're definitely acting strange right now," Max says.

"Jerk," I whisper back, voice harsh. I can't believe we are having an elementary school fight over the fact that I didn't sit with him a couple of times.

"Weirdo."

I slow down, leaving some distance from the rest of the group. "Butt face," I hiss.

"Butt face?" he asks.

"I said what I said."

He sighs. "Can we just hang out again? I know making friends is important, but we should have each other's backs." He pauses. "It's okay if it's hard now. We haven't had to make new friends in a long time."

It's not like the two of us are antisocial. I know a bunch of people at school through the drama department and our Science Olympiad team, and Max was briefly in a band. Even if it's been a while since I made a deep friendship, it's not like I'm incapable of doing it again.

I fold my arms across my chest. "It's certainly not hard for me; I'm already close with Saron." We did have breakfast and then sit together on the bus, so it counts.

"Well, that was fast. Good for you, Tal. It's still hard for me." He starts to walk ahead of me, closer to the rest of the group.

At first, I think, *Good. Walk away.* But once the initial anger fades, I start to worry. It's hard for him?

I rub the bead on my fidget ring.

"Moxie, wait," I say.

He turns his head a little to look at me and then slows down.

"You're right. I'm a weirdo," I say.

"Finally coming to your senses. Accepting the truth is the first step."

"Toward what exactly?"

"Toward overcoming the weirdness."

I roll my eyes. "Want to sit together on the bus?" I ask.

"I don't know. I was actually watching *Finding Dory* with a couple of the guys in the back of the bus, and we're sort of in the middle of the movie, so . . ."

"Ugh, you're the worst," I say.

We spend the rest of the hike together, walking side by side.

GETTING TO KNOW YOU

It's rafting time. I'm not sure if rafting is seasonally appropriate, but somehow here we are. Honestly, compared to back home, it does feel super warm. Plus, I think this is one of those mandatory things most tour groups to Israel end up doing. Which is why, by the time Chaya tells us to separate into five groups and put on life jackets, I've decided this will actually be fun.

Picking out the right size jacket is the worst. I wrap my arms over my stomach, my hands settled on the side cutouts of my bright yellow bathing suit. I should have never allowed Cat to talk me into buying it. I can feel the elastic along the side cutting into my skin. It probably looks like my flesh is bursting out of the open spaces.

If I put on the extra-large life jacket, it might slip off, and then I'll drown. I mean, I know how to swim, sure, but what if I hit my head on a rock and the life jacket is so big that the current just takes it right off me? I could definitely drown then. If I take the large size one and it won't close, then I will be deeply embarrassed forever, so there's really no winning.

Saron walks over and grabs a medium women's life jacket, buckles it with ease, and then walks away.

I go to touch my fidget ring but then remember I left it in my day bag with my change of clothes and towel for safe-keeping. I'm being ridiculous. I grab the extra-large life jacket and walk over to where Saron and Max are standing.

I snap the buckles together. The jacket is loose, but it's fine. I'll just adjust the straps to make them a little tighter.

"Hey, Tal, have you met Joshua and Gabriel yet?" Max asks when I get closer. He waves toward the two boys he was with on the bus, and I realize they're the ones who were taking pictures with the #IVEGOTCHUTZPAH banner.

They introduce themselves. Gabriel is about the same height as Max but lankier. He's got a hi-top fade so perfect that it looks like he got it done just before the trip. He's standing perfectly straight and still while Joshua, right by his side, is rocking on the balls of his feet. Joshua is half a foot shorter with close-cropped strawberry-blond hair set on top of his unusually round head. He has a streak of sunscreen across his cheeks, with an additional blob over his nose, that he hasn't properly rubbed in.

"Do you guys have any rafting experience?" I ask.

"Not at all—I haven't even been swimming in years. This is going to be awesome!" Joshua says in a rush.

"I'm on the swim team at school," Gabriel says. His

cadence is slower than Joshua's, like his words are more deliberate. "I'll make sure he doesn't die."

It turns out there's nothing to be worried about. The water is so shallow that it's barely above my ankles as I climb onto the raft.

"So you two know each other?" Gabriel asks, pointing to Max and me as he takes his seat.

"Met in utero. Twins," I say.

"I thought you two were dating," Joshua says as he takes a step onto the raft.

Gabriel puts his head in his hands. "You can't say that," he tells his friend.

"What? I didn't know!" Joshua defends himself. "That would be super gross, though. It would be incest, you know? Wait. It would be . . . twincest," Joshua continues.

Gabriel doesn't take his head out of his hands.

Saron sighs. "Am I the only one who came alone? Joshua and Gabriel are friends; Tally and Max are siblings. I should have forced someone to accompany me."

"I'm here alone," says Sammy, walking up to our group. "Mind if I join you all?"

"Please do; now I won't be outnumbered," Saron says. "I claim Sammy," she adds, turning to us. "You pre-trip friends can go screw yourselves, 'cause we're starting a girl gang and you're not allowed in."

Gabriel and Sammy start with the oars, guiding our raft along the shallow water. We bump up against a branch within the first couple of minutes, and Sammy has to jab her oar against a rock to get us out of the jam.

"So," I start, looking over at Joshua and Gabriel, sitting near each other. "You two go to school together, right?"

"Even better," Joshua says. "We're JV lacrosse co-captains."

"How does that make it better?" Saron asks. Her tone makes it clear this is not an actual question.

"I'm not really a sports person," I cut in. "But I know they can really help you get into schools. College applications can be so out of control now. Sammy, you said you applied to what—fourteen schools? Do you play any sports?"

"Yeah," she says. "I run track. Not sure if it will help; I wasn't in a position to get recruited or anything."

"I love running," Saron says. "Organized sports, less so. But give me a treadmill and some music and I'm all set."

"Oh! What's your fastest mile?" Sammy asks.

This is not going as planned. The two of them start talking about the best sneakers and cute yet durable athletic wear and running playlists.

The whole *not talking about college applications* thing would be okay if Max were at least contributing to the conversation. Instead, he's sitting silently, looking out at the sparse trees and dry grass bordering the water. With his face turned, all I can see is the scar over his eyebrow, looking particularly red in the sun. This feels like a bad sign.

He takes the oars from Sammy when she claims her arms have been turned into noodles. I watch them as they make the exchange, trying to track the subtlety of their glances and whether their fingers touch.

"Thanks," Sammy says softly to Max, looking directly into his eyes.

He gives her a half smile.

"Oh! I want to try," Joshua calls out so loudly from the front of the raft that I whip my head around to look at him.

"Just don't drop it," Gabriel warns. He gets up carefully so Joshua can take his seat.

"Why would I drop it?" Joshua asks, plopping down into the open spot with such force that the whole raft wobbles. "The thing you have to understand is that I have sticky fingers. Not like I steal things but sticky like a spider. Like I'm Spider-Man," he says as he drops the oar into the water. "Oh."

I glance back at Max and Sammy as Joshua tries to retrieve the oar, but the moment has passed. Sammy is talking to Saron about a book she just finished reading, and Max is trying to hold the raft in place so we don't drift away without Joshua.

It's fine; I can try again later.

≡ ———— ≡

After rafting, we change back into our normal clothes, get back on the bus, and make a pit stop to get some food before we head to the winery. I didn't even know they had wineries in Israel.

The bus stops in what looks like an abandoned shopping center. There's a McDonald's and a grocery store that appear to still be open, but the rest of the structure looks worn down. It gets even worse when we are inside, all flickering lights and empty stores, one of which just has a half-built mannequin in it. Very creepy.

"Grocery store?" Saron asks, already walking toward the entrance. Sammy, Max, and I follow. We've lost Joshua and Gabriel to the McDonald's.

As we start searching for food, I give it another shot. "Saron, have you applied to any schools yet? You mentioned something about an application portfolio."

"Yeah, finishing up the supplemental material now. I'm applying exclusively to design programs," she adds.

"Stop it! That is so cool," Sammy says. "Who's your favorite designer?"

"You can't ask me to pick just one; that's cruel."

We turn into the snack aisle. The section looks the same as the snack aisle in my suburban grocery store, with the notable exception that I don't recognize any of the brands and everything is written in Hebrew. Jess is standing near the chocolate bars.

"Hey, what are you folks up to?"

"We were talking about college applications," I say. I glance over at Max, who is silently looking at the row of chips in front of him.

"Were we?" Saron asks.

"Where did you go to school, Jess?" I continue.

"Oh, I didn't," she says. "Wasn't my path."

Saron groans. "Tally Mark," she says, "we're in Israel. Let's just appreciate this moment and these snacks without any boring school talk."

I'm being boring. *Great.*

"Anyway," Jess cuts in, "I can run an impromptu tutorial on Israeli snacks if you want. Like this one, you have to buy it; trust me," she says, pointing to a bar of chocolate with a red wrapper and a cow on it. There are some words on it in Hebrew that I can't read. "And these—wait—no one is allergic to peanuts, right? This is Bamba, and it's basically what happens if you took the cheese out of cheese puffs and substituted it with peanut butter."

"Oh, I love those. I ate so much Bamba the last time I was here," Sammy says.

"You've been to Israel before?" I ask.

"Oh, yeah. With family. We visited for each bat mitzvah. Three girls; I'm in the middle," she explains.

She keeps kosher, works at her JCC, and has been to Israel three times . . . and I don't even know if we have a local Jewish Community Center and I've never been to Israel. I bet she doesn't know the history as well as I do, though.

I need to stop comparing us; it's not like it's a competition. I shouldn't be making this an imaginary test on Jewishness.

"I bet you're jealous I claimed her now," Saron says, looking over at Max and me. She puts her arm around Sammy's shoulder. "You can be the brains of the girl gang because of your insider Israeli knowledge. I'm the brawn, beauty, and bark."

This isn't a friendship competition, either, I tell myself.

When we're back on the bus, Jess convinces us to try out the chocolate.

"Let it just sit on your tongue. Don't bite it." Jess has this sly smile on her adorable grandma face.

The chocolate is good, sweet and creamy. I'm not sure what Jess is waiting for, though. It starts to melt on my tongue and—

"Oh!" I say, surprised. "What is that?" The chocolate is popping. *Popping.*

"It's basically Pop Rocks chocolate," Jess says excitedly. "Good surprise, right?"

I laugh. It *is* actually delicious. Once the popping has stopped, I break off another piece. I think about how Saron told me to appreciate this moment and these snacks.

At least I can appreciate the chocolate.

LA VIE BOHÈME

I stare out the window as we drive to the winery. I can't get over how everything appears empty and sprawling and covered in dirt. Back home, there are so many more brushes of green and blue and gray, muted and cold colors, but the whole color palette of Israel is different, all shades of yellow and beige, broken only occasionally by greenery. Admittedly, for part of the way, we are on a highway, which isn't all that different from back home, except the signs are in Hebrew, Arabic, and English.

It doesn't take us long to get to the winery, and everyone who's eighteen seems pretty excited. After the tour, we get to go to a wine tasting, while the young'uns get to try out some local cheeses. Even Saron, who is sitting next to me, literally claps her hands together when the bus stops.

I look at Max. We should stay behind.

I've always felt weird around alcohol. It just doesn't make

sense to me why people would want to lose control. I crave control. I fight anxiety brain all the time just to get some semblance of it.

Like right now, as my brain tells me that if we go inside the winery and I don't drink, people will hate me like Burr hates Hamilton in "Your Obedient Servant." I'm not necessarily saying that they'll challenge me to a duel, but I can't rule it out.

Then there's Max. I know he drinks sometimes, but the last time that happened, he decided to get in the car with someone else who had, too. There's just too much pressure in this stop for the both of us.

Max walks off the bus like everything is fine, though, so I follow.

We head into what looks like a wine shop merged with a welcome center. There's a big desk and maps around the walls that show where they grow their grapes. There are rows and rows of bottled wine, which make me think of *The Parent Trap*, because the dad in the movie has his own winery, and Lindsay Lohan gets to live there after she switches with the other Lindsay Lohan.

Apparently, we're getting a new guide, just for the winery. "My favorite," Chaya says. An older man with a blue-and-silver yarmulke on his head walks over to her, slightly hunched. "Shalom," Chaya greets. She gives the man a hug.

It turns out his name *is* Shalom, which is kind of like meeting someone named Hello. "Shalom" technically also means "peace," which is nice, actually.

"Come, children, come," he says, shepherding us through a set of glass doors to the left of the welcome desk. I'm expecting some sort of sprawling field of grapes, but instead there are these huge machines that look like silos out on a farm and a couple of warehouses.

We walk into one of the warehouses, and it's absolutely packed with barrels. Rows and rows of them. There's even an empty one propped up on a stand so we can see what it looks like inside.

"Yes. Here. We stop." Shalom leans against a railing and waits for us to gather around him.

Shalom talks about how they grow their grapes at different elevations within Israel (apparently this helps them make different kinds of wine) and the unique effect of different woods and the fermentation process. We walk back outside, and he shows us the silo structures again, which are actually huge aeration machines. It's cool, from a technical point of view.

Then he announces it's time to drink.

"All right, under eighteens, come with me," Jess says.

This is my chance. I'll just grab Max, and we can head to the other activity with Joshua and Gabriel and the rest of the younger crew.

He walks inside the tasting room.

Well, then. I can't leave him alone now, so I guess I'm going to the wine tasting.

There's a special room just for this with a big circular bar. We spread out.

We're instructed on how to properly savor the wine, including a full demonstration from Shalom where he shows us how to swirl the wine, sniff it, and take tiny sips to savor the robust flavors, before the samples are poured.

I notice Max shake his head when the attendant comes around to his spot, his hand placed over the wineglass.

I'm still watching him from the other side of the counter. He walked in next to Sammy, and they're talking now. He smiles. I wonder what he's saying.

I don't notice when the wine attendant pours a sample into my own cup.

"Want mine?" I ask David. He's standing next to me, swirling his wine around in its glass, just like Shalom showed us.

"You trying to liquor me up?"

"Caught," I say. "And I thought I was so sneaky."

"You don't drink?" he asks.

I shake my head.

"Cool. I didn't start until college. Someone decided to teach me beer pong, and then that did not go well, so I didn't try it again for a few weeks. Moderation and all that."

"So is that a no?"

"Oh, yeah, actually I probably shouldn't have yours. You keep forgetting I need to be responsible. I'm in charge of keeping everyone safe here."

"How's that going?"

"I took a very informative self-defense class last night, so it's going pretty well, thanks for asking." He tries to replicate the eyes/groin move I did last night.

Saron, standing at my other side, looks over, confused. "Did the boy just have a seizure?"

"Nah, he's refusing extra wine and attempting self-defense," I explain.

"Extra wine? Oh, I'll help with that." She picks up my glass and downs it.

"Aren't you supposed to let it settle on your tongue and waft through your palate?" I ask.

"Oh, babe, you're cute." She pats the top of my head. "I'll take the rest of them too."

After a few more samples, we're dismissed to the store. We're allowed to buy one bottle, if we so wish. Saron has me buy one for her, too, because she wants more of *that dessert one*.

It's as everyone is picking out their bottles that I find Max. He's standing alone, next to a row of red wine. It almost looks like he's contemplating buying a bottle.

"Hey," I say softly. "You okay?"

He looks over at me. "Sure. Why?"

What does he want me to say? *Because you almost died in a drunk-driving accident?*

Instead, I shrug. "Just checking in."

"You?" he asks.

"I'm great."

He nods.

We go back to the bus.

This should be it, since, according to our itinerary, the next stop is our hostel.

Chaya doesn't get in her seat. Instead, she stands in the middle of the aisle and claps her hands together.

"Surprise," she says. "We are going to visit an artist studio, and then we are going to the hostel! He lives in Tzfat, the artist colony, not far, and there will be a talk about Kabbalah, Jewish mysticism!"

I feel like the day is turning around now. An artist who specializes in Jewish mysticism? I don't even know what that means.

But I'm ready for some inspiration.

ONE SONG GLORY

I'm sitting in a white plastic foldout chair with my musical notebook open on my lap.

We were told to gather in an area that was converted into a small classroom. There's art all over the walls and chairs neatly lined up in rows. To get here, you have to walk through a gift shop, absolutely crowded with prints and postcards. Some members of our group are still looking through the store, slowly milling into the classroom.

It seems odd to host a lecture in this space. Despite the art, despite the chairs, it's clear that this is just a house, one of many lined up along the cobbled road, identical stone buildings so old and quaint that they look like they belong in a documentary on medieval times.

I tap my pen against the blank page.

"Are you writing again?" Max asks.

I shrug. "Trying." I run my fingers over the edge of

the notebook so that the pages fan out. "Did you bring yours?"

"I did, actually," he says softly. "It's at the hostel."

"You can borrow mine," I offer quickly. "In case you're moved by the art and want to jot something down."

He shakes his head. "Not feeling particularly moved."

I want to say something else, maybe tell him it's okay that he isn't feeling inspired yet . . . that I'm not either. That we have a whole trip ahead of us, days left for that to change.

Before I can talk, Joshua plops down in the seat next to me. "Oh, hey! Are you a writer?" he asks, grabbing my notebook.

"Give it back," Gabriel says, voice tired.

Joshua drops my notebook unceremoniously back in my lap. "Sorry! I just love writing!" he says.

"Do *you* write?" I ask.

"Oh, no. Not a creative bone in my body. I volunteer at our school library, and when you're surrounded by books, you just get emotionally close to the written word, you know?"

I guess I feel the same way about music and theater, even if my connection *is* linked to creativity. Even if that creativity has abandoned me now.

"So do you write?" he continues, voice cheery again. "Maybe someday I can shelve your book!"

"I don't write like that," I explain. "I'm more of a lyricist. Max too," I add. "But I go for musicals, and he goes for alternative indie folk soft rock."

"Not what it's called," Max says.

"A musician," Sammy says, sitting down in the seat in front of Max. "I like that," she adds, looking directly at Max. Then she turns in her chair to face the front, her long black hair draped across the back of the seat.

I swear I can see Max blush.

The rest of the group filters into the room. Saron walks in and joins Sammy in her row, sitting in the spot right in front of me. She promptly takes her sketch pad out of her bag.

"Hoping to get some inspiration from the talk?" I ask.

She practically snorts in response. "Not exactly my brand of art," she says. The colors in the room are bright, almost cartoonlike. Nothing like the sharp lines and muted colors I saw in Saron's sketch this morning.

From the way her paper is angled, I can see her start a new silhouette: a mermaid dress. By the time the lecture starts, she's working on a careful design of vines along the neckline.

If Saron can work during the lecture, then maybe I can too. I leave my notebook open as we hear all about the significance of the number eight in Jewish mysticism and the power of the all-seeing-eye design, both of which play prominently in the brightly colored paintings lining the walls.

Maybe I can write about that. Eight rhymes with great. The great eight. Never late. Relies on fate. Choose love, not hate.

Ugh. What am I, some clichéd Dr. Seuss? This isn't going to work.

I used to write with Cat. She'd come up with some

over-the-top pitch for a musical and I'd try to write songs to fit the story, or we'd start with one of my songs and build the rest around it. When writer's block hit, no suggestion or story proved strong enough to break through. Not even when she proposed a musical reimagining of *Good Omens*, which, like, objectively was brilliant and should have worked.

So now it's on me.

I could give up, I guess. That would be easier. Except giving up feels like a betrayal, letting go of years of hard work we put into our music.

I miss that feeling when the words click. That's another reason why I can't give up, the warm pride of reading something I just wrote and knowing that it's mine. I created that.

I wonder when I'm going to feel that again.

I close the notebook. I'll try again later.

≡ —————— ≡

We have some downtime before dinner.

I run through my plan. I'll go to Max's room so we can call our parents before we head to the dining area. If his temporary roommate is there, we can just go in the hall, still under the guise of talking to our family. Before we reach out to them, I'll casually bring up our new friends on the trip. When we get to Sammy, I'll let it slip that she thinks he's cute, then top it off with something like, "Oh! Don't tell her I told you that!" Then I'll just sit back and watch him fluster and fumble his way into being normal.

Then I guess we can call Mom and Dad for real.

I open up my messages, thinking about sending them a heads-up that we might call, but something catches my eye.

Cat: THIS BETTER BE INSPIRING YOU! YOU OWE ME SONGS. still not talking to you kay love you hun

I can read the text in her voice, so clearly it's like she's right next to me. I put it out of my head.

I still don't have any new lyrics, except for the eight/great thing. Which doesn't really count.

I put my phone into my purse without sending anything to Mom and Dad. Maybe it would be better to surprise them.

I head toward Max's room, hopeful as I walk closer to his door.

Until I hear the crying.

No. No, this can't be happening. Today didn't go that terribly, did it? He's making friends; we talked a little bit about college. We were around art.

He can't be crying, not now.

I can hear muffled sobs coming from inside his room. The door is propped open by the lock; his roommate probably left it that way. I doubt Max even knows anyone can hear him.

I peek inside, and it's definitely Max, sitting at the edge of the bed. He's hunched over something, weeping. I squint. It's his notebook; he's crying over his notebook.

Which makes it even worse.

Not only is Max still sad, but he's crying over something I brought up. I thought asking about his music would help. I really did.

I walk away, careful not to let him see me, because I don't want to embarrass him.

Now I'm even more worried than before. We are nearing the end of day two in Israel—day three of our trip, if you count the time on the plane—and I'm not making things better.

I'm failing. And now I'm crying too.

ANYBODY HAVE A MAP?

The worst part about crying outside a hostel in Israel at the end of December is the wind. I forgot my jacket, and the air is sharp enough to raise goose bumps along my arms.

I absentmindedly rub my forearms.

Cat used to play this game where she would ask me, *What's the worst thing that could happen?* I always knew what she wanted me to say—something along the lines of, "Oh, this problem is small and I'm overthinking things; thank you so much for your wisdom!" Except the thing with anxiety brain is that I can always imagine something catastrophic, and it feels completely real and possible.

But maybe tonight, the thought path will work. *What's the worst thing that could happen?* I ask myself. Max misses the BU application deadline. Everything I thought for years was a guarantee is ruined. I still go to school, but I'm alone.

I linger on that feeling of loneliness, so heavy that I feel the physical weight in my lungs. I see myself sitting in an empty dorm room before walking aimlessly through campus as people pass me by. I have no one to talk to, nowhere to go. I am completely isolated.

No, I can't be alone; I won't allow it.

Except I'm alone now. And it's my own fault.

I should be inside, enjoying myself, but instead I'm sitting in the cold picturing my lonely, desperate future. I'm missing out; I'm always missing out; I can't enjoy anything; I can't—

"Well, now, what are you doing here, Tally Mark?"

I look up and see Saron walking over. She hands me a plate and sits down on the grass next to me.

"I noticed you weren't at dinner," she says. "Brought you the goods."

"Thanks," I say, accepting a plate of lukewarm spaghetti.

She squints at me in the darkness. "Is everything okay?"

Is my face red? Puffy? Can she tell that I was just crying? She can probably tell, and now she thinks I'm weird. And she's right—I *am* weird. I'm totally weird and totally not okay.

I feel that heaviness in my lungs again, and before I know what's happening, I blurt out, "Max was in a car accident."

"*What?*" Saron looks around, like she might see the crash in the mountains.

"Over the summer," I clarify. "He's fine now. Physically fine, I mean. I just . . . I don't know; this is silly. I thought that this trip might help him feel better, and I don't think it is."

Saron nods. "Come on, we can talk about it in my room. You're shivering."

Am I? I can feel my jaw wobble, hear the sound of my teeth tap together. I wonder if it's from the cold or from the nerves.

I follow Saron to her room, still holding the plate of spaghetti. When we get there, she sits on her hostel bed.

"Where's your roommate?" I ask, sitting down next to her.

"I lucked into something quite extraordinary," Saron says, taking out the bottle of wine from her bag. "My roommate is yet another person here with a friend. I've seen her, like, twice; she keeps going to her friend's room. I have to believe they'll demand to be roomed together in our next place."

I nod, not really sure what else to do. It's too quiet right now. I should probably say something. Especially because she's opening up the bottle of wine, and I don't want to have the embarrassing conversation about how I don't drink because of my anxiety. Instead of watching her, I take my hair out of my ponytail and then put it back in an identical ponytail. That's not distracting enough, so I play with my fidget ring, first rubbing the bead, then twisting the whole ring around my finger.

Saron doesn't seem to notice. She got a corkscrew at the winery with her bottle and is trying to figure out how to use it. I watch as she pulls the cork out, triumphant.

"Want some?" she asks.

I shake my head.

"You said earlier you don't drink, right? Much more disciplined than I am," she says.

"Oh, I don't have that much discipline," I say. "You should see me with coffee."

She smiles. "I like a girl who knows her vices."

I notice her sketch pad, balanced on top of her suitcase. The mermaid dress is now decorated, first with a line of vines, then grapes, then barrels. By the legs, she's drawn a row of bottles, one of which is uncorked and upside down, just above the flare of the dress. The bottom juts out in reds and purples. She's written a little note next to it that just reads: *tulle?*

Clearly she was inspired by the winery. I wonder what the political commentary is here; maybe the wine at the bottom is supposed to look similar to the blood in her last sketch?

"All right, so Max," she starts. "What's our goal? What are we working toward?"

"Um." I twirl a strand of spaghetti on my fork. I can tell Saron everything right now; I told her part of it already. *What's the worst thing that could happen?*

"I just want to see him happy." That's part of the truth, at least.

"Well, what makes him happy?"

I could list all the things I've already tried, but instead I say, "I think he might like Sammy."

Saron sits up straight. "Wait. Wait, I just came up with the smartest idea to ever exist."

"I'm scared to ask what that is," I say.

"We're going to set them up, Tally Mark," she says. "We're going to be matchmakers."

"Both of us?"

"Of course," she says. "You wouldn't know it by just talking to me, but I have played matchmaker in the past. It's one of my favorite pastimes. Have you ever read *Emma*?"

"By Jane Austen?" I ask.

"Yes, *Emma*. We're going to pull an *Emma*."

I take a breath so deep, it fills my lungs. I can't believe Saron is going to help me with Max.

"Okay, and how does one *pull an* Emma?"

"They follow me," she says and then waggles her eyebrows. "Thank goodness you met me on this trip, Tally Mark. I'm going to make things a lot more fun around here. We're going to set people up; we're going to adventure. I'd be shocked if I don't give you a makeover by the end of this trip, just for the hell of it. I see a bright future for the two of us," she says.

"As matchmakers?" I ask.

She shakes her head. "No, Tally Mark. As friends."

MATCHMAKER

The day begins with the Israelis.

Chaya preps us on the bus. She says it's called a Mifgash, or an encounter. There's going to be five Israelis joining our group tomorrow. They'll be with us for a few days before they have to get back to normal things, like school and living their lives. Then, in a few months, they'll be traveling to the States, and we'll get to show them around.

"Not everyone understands the English language as well, so just try to speak slower. Welcome them. They will be part of the group today."

The bus stops, and we all mill about in what seems like a random parking lot. Honestly, no clue why they picked this place for our big Mifgash Moment, but here we are.

Chaya goes to gather the Israelis, leaving Jess and David in charge. Which basically means David is doing a poor job organizing us all until Jess gets exasperated and takes over.

When Chaya comes back, accompanied by the Israelis, she says, "Hello, yes, over here. We will make the introductions, get to know one another a little better."

Our new trip mates are as follows:

Etan: 17

"I'd like to show him my Promised Land." —Saron, who I now suspect might still be a little drunk from last night? If that's even possible?

Shira: 18

"I'd like to show her my Promised Land." —Jess

Rivkah: 18

Waves shyly when introduced, immediately endearing.

Eli: 16

Dressed like he's trying to sneak into a frat party.

Amit: 17

Looks like he could be cast as the romantic lead in a musical about bodybuilders.

After Chaya gives us her brief introductions, she puts us into groups to get to know one another. Then, for the purposes of bonding and making us look ridiculous, she tells us to come up with team names and a secret handshake.

This Cultural Exchange Moment™ will be brought to you by Embarrassment. Available now, in stores worldwide.

"The handshake will be easy. Max and I memorized the one from *The Parent Trap*; we can teach you all," I say to our little group. Rivkah has joined Saron, Sammy, Max, Joshua, Gabriel, and me.

"Our mom thought we'd like it because it's about twins," Max explains. "So, naturally, we watched it so many times that we memorized the over-the-top handshake. We're really good at it too," he adds, proud.

"I'm not even going to touch the levels of weird going on here, but fine," says Saron.

"We still need a name, though," Gabriel points out.

"Easy. The Jew Crew," Saron says.

"We can't be called the Jew Crew," I say.

"I don't know . . . it feels right," Saron says.

We're running out of time. Chaya comes around and says that she wants us to present in a few minutes. Max and I decide that it will be cooler if Rivkah joins in on the special handshake, so we try to very quickly teach her. We make great first impressions.

Each group does a little presentation of their handshake. I mean, we rock ours, and Saron has roughly zero shame in announcing that we are the Jew Crew. She says it so confidently that I'm almost on board.

There's no real winning or losing here because the point is bonding in mutual awkwardness. Though we clearly won.

David walks over as we are making our way back to the bus and says, *"Parent Trap?"*

I smile. "Can't confirm or deny."

$$\Longrightarrow \text{————} \Longleftarrow$$

Our next stop is Tel Aviv. This morning we have a street-art tour of the city and then lunch in a Tel Aviv shuk.

Saron and I have a plan for both stops.

We worked it out last night, and I have to say it's brilliant. We're staging a multifaceted love attack, based on Saron's key steps to romance: proximity and alone time. Chaya has promised us there is some sort of surprise in the afternoon. You can't plan for a surprise, so we'll have to think on our feet for that one.

Saron is excited for the street-art tour and not just because of the proximity section of our matchmaking plan.

"Do you know how often street art is belittled?" she asks as we make our way to the tour. "People just don't see it as Real Art with a capital 'R' and 'A,' you know? Like, just because it isn't framed in some museum, it doesn't count. Which is obviously wrong. I mean, street art is making some of the biggest strides, all while providing vital social commentaries. It's not just Banksy, 'cause, like, that's all anyone knows about street art; they know Banksy."

I nod.

"You're going to love this tour. I know it. You're going to immediately decide to major in street art once this is done," she continues.

"Is that a thing you can major in?" I ask.

"It should be," Saron says. "Which is exactly the point."

We're standing in a small park that is, for some reason, in the middle of a road. I guess people in a city have to fit in greenery wherever they can. The lines of grass are split by a paved walkway for pedestrians. Wooden benches sit at the edge of the park, backed by a line of trees that I think were strategically placed to provide shade. Saron is leaning with her whole back against one of the trees closest to our group.

When our street-art tour guide arrives, she gathers us on the paved walkway, which is directly in the sun. Even with sunscreen on, I'm sure I'll have a slight burn by the end of this trip. The new guide is small and enthusiastic. She's got hot-pink hair, braided with strands of gold. Someone had to have helped her do that this morning. There's no way I could do something as intricate as that alone.

"Welcome, American friends!" she says. "I am Dvora. I lead the cool tours of street art. I'm an artist myself. Oh, maybe we even see my art." She raises an eyebrow. "We'll see. Now, come, friends! Let us start!"

Yes, let us start.

"Wouldn't it be funny," Saron poses to our little group of friends, "if we tried to act out all the street art?" Just as planned.

I shrug. "The pictures might be cool."

"That could be fun," Max says.

"I'm in," Sammy adds.

Thank goodness. This plan hinges on their participation. The first few pictures we take are pretty standard. Some silly faces, pretending to blend in to a couple of abstract backgrounds. Saron acts as the photographer because she brought a real camera with her. This also places one of us in a position to dole out the modeling roles.

Our hope for this part of the plan is that at least one of the pictures will involve a couple in some sort of close embrace. We luck into something even better.

"We need a couple to kiss," Saron says. "I don't make the rules; I just follow the art."

She's stopped in front of a piece with a scantily clad woman and a man in a suit. The woman looks like she's on display, which I think might be the point. The man, meanwhile, is in professional attire with a briefcase at his feet. Their lips are touching, but the rest of their bodies seem distant, curved away from each other.

"We could," Joshua suggests, waving to Gabriel. He's wearing the #IVEGOTCHUTZPAH banner wrapped around his waist like a large belt that's held together by a hair clip, which was graciously provided by Sammy.

Saron's eyes get very big, like she's considering the proposal. She looks at me. "The whole point of this picture is to question toxic heteronormative standards. We'll find you two a more artistically authentic reason to make out. Sammy and Max should take this one."

Gabriel blushes. So does Sammy.

"Oh, I don't know," Sammy starts.

"Come on, you practically look like the girl in the picture; it's perfect casting," Saron says.

This is not technically true per se. First of all, the woman in the picture is just a black-and-white outline in a short, tight dress, with her hair piled high atop her head. Sammy, meanwhile, is wearing a loose maxi dress with a crew neck and sleeves just past her elbows. She has her long black hair down, underneath a pale-pink baseball cap.

She still goes up to the wall and stands directly next to the work of art. Max follows.

At this point, most of our group has moved on to the next building. "You all coming?" Jess asks. "I can't be responsible for losing six members of our group, but I also want to see the rest of the tour."

"Almost done," Saron assures her, lining up the shot. "Whenever you two are ready," she says to Max and Sammy.

Max leans over and whispers something into Sammy's ear. She laughs and then nods. He bends down to kiss her cheek and holds the pose, their bodies otherwise arched away from each other, just like in the picture behind them.

"Guys, come on," Jess says. "Group. Tour. Gotta keep up."

Saron glances quickly at me and then shrugs. It's not perfect, but it's something. She takes the picture.

After the tour, we head to the Tel Aviv shuk. The market here is much bigger than the one in Jaffa. While that had the feeling of a yard sale, all foldout tables and unorganized goods, this is a standard open-air market. Each stall looks official, like a store cut open to let in more light and then stretched vertically so that it can practically reach the sky. I see a stall with touristy T-shirts, boasting our location and sporting Hebrew phrases, another covered in colorful jewelry. There's a whole table with nothing but cell phone cases. It looks hectic and bright and bursting with life.

It's absolutely packed in the market, which is perfect for the next step in our master matchmaking plan: alone time. While it's great that they're bonding around all of us, there's no way anything serious is going to go down in a big group.

We have to be especially careful with this one because it's basically what Max called me out on earlier. Ditching him, that is. We can't have a repeat of the weirdo debacle. So our evil plan is to make it look like an accident.

"I think we need an Israeli," Joshua says before we enter the shuk.

"Just any Israeli?" Gabriel asks.

"No, dude. One of our Israelis. We need to snag an Israeli and integrate them into the Jew Crew," Joshua says.

"Oh, please tell me we aren't sticking with that name," I say.

Joshua ignores me and continues. "Rivkah was in the original group. We could just get her to join us again." Without waiting for our response, he turns to look through the rest of the group. We're crowded on the sidewalk just outside the market, waiting for Chaya to tell us when and where we need to meet up post-lunch. "Rivkah," he yells out.

"Has anyone seen— Oh! There she is." He makes a beeline for her. She looks pretty confused, but she still walks over to join us.

Which ends up being perfect because she knows some of the best places to get food in the shuk. She takes us to this place that serves bourekas, which is fried dough that can be filled with mashed potatoes. You can even add an egg. It's the most delicious combo I never knew I needed in my life. As we're eating, she mentions that there is a smoothie place at the end of the market.

"Close to the . . . eh . . . place we meet," she says.

I look over at Saron. This is exactly the sort of thing we need.

"Oh, that's perfect," I say. "We could make that our meeting spot, just in case anyone gets separated. Head there as soon as we're finished eating these." I wave the small paper bag with the yummy mashed potato dough. I got mine in the first batch of bourekas, but Gabriel and Sammy are still waiting for theirs.

"It really is hectic in here," Saron says. "Good to make a plan, just in case."

We're almost too good at this.

Or at least we were until we can't seem to separate the group. We didn't really factor in Joshua and Gabriel. Or Rivkah, for that matter. They're all being way too considerate. Gabriel keeps looking over his shoulder to make sure we are all still together as we move through the crowds of locals and tourists.

"What're we going to do?" I whisper to Saron. I have to get really close for her to hear because it's that freaking packed and loud. It feels like everyone in Israel has crammed into this market and they're all talking at once.

She doesn't answer. I'm a little worried that maybe she didn't hear me because of the noise, so the plan is going to fail because we can't give Max and Sammy alone time. Or that she did hear me and she's decided she hates me now.

She tugs Sammy's arm.

"Oh, look at these," she says.

We're standing in front of a stall that is completely decked out in jewelry. Earrings, bracelets, necklaces, all featuring either a Star of David or a hamsa, the protective hand design. They're made out of different materials, some with beads, some in gold, some out of woven thread.

"I think I might want to get something for my mom. What do you think?" Saron asks.

I squeeze into the spot next to the two of them, away from the moving crowd that is pushing through the area between the stalls. I'm not sure why Saron just pulled aside Sammy, when we need the two of them together.

Except Max is still with us. Did he? Did he wait for Sammy? Oh, this is so cute. He definitely does like her. I knew that blush yesterday meant something; he must have seen Saron pull Sammy aside and stopped so he could stay close to her.

Max catches my eye. He skirts around the crowd so he can stand next to me. "Do you think we should pick anything up for Mom and Dad?" he asks.

"Oh, yeah, probably," I say. "I'm not sure anything here is speaking to me."

"We can keep looking," Saron interjects. Then she makes a show of turning around and looking at each of us. "Where'd everyone else go?" she asks.

"Lost them," Max says.

"I guess it's good we came up with that meeting-spot idea," Saron says. "Shall we move on?"

Now it's just the four of us, which makes it significantly easier to execute our plan. Saron waits for them to get a little ahead of us before she pulls me into another stall, this one filled with Bohemian dresses. "Duck," she says.

We crouch down behind one of the racks, perfectly hidden by the long, flowy dresses. There's no way they'll be able to see us.

"What are you two doing?" someone asks.

I look up. Jess is standing right next to the rack, holding one of the dresses.

Saron hushes her. "Get down here," she adds.

Jess raises an eyebrow. Then she shrugs and crouches down next to us.

"Is there a reason why . . . ?" she starts.

Saron turns her head to look directly at me. "Tally Mark," she says, "this is a defining moment in our matchmaking career. I think we should bring Jess into the so-called fold. It could be helpful having someone on the inside." Without waiting for my response, she looks over at Jess. "We're trying to set up Tally's brother with Sammy. He needs it, emotionally speaking."

"Oh," Jess says. "You're pulling an *Emma*."

Saron's face lights up. "Exactly."

"How does hiding behind a bunch of dresses help set them up?" Jess asks.

"Alone time," I explain.

Jess nods. "Obviously."

Saron makes us wait for exactly two minutes before she deems it safe enough to get up. "Should we actually look for gifts now?" she asks.

We have half an hour before we need to meet up with the big group, which means that we still have time before we should get to the smoothie place. We look at some gifts, and Jess ends up getting this big, floppy straw hat for herself. I buy a new mezuzah for my parents, because the one at our front door is getting a little worn and they'll probably think it's cool to have a customary case with verses from the Torah that comes directly from Israel (even though the one I bought was actually pretty cheap).

I see Sammy and Max before we get to the smoothie booth. She's leaning against a light post, just outside the market, a red smoothie in her hand. She holds it out to Max. He takes a sip.

He looks so happy.

When we reach the smoothie place, I turn to Saron. "This one's on me," I say, holding up my wallet. "We're celebrating."

UNDER THE SEA

It turns out that our afternoon surprise is a trip to the beach.

This was greeted by a lot of excitement from us Northeast teens. The Israelis seem far more skeptical. Rivkah put on a sweatshirt before we even left the bus.

The Tel Aviv beach is nothing like the beaches I'm used to going to in Massachusetts. The city creeps up to the shoreline, separated by a road and a stretch of sand. It looks too metropolitan for bathing suits and salty water, like a glitch in the system forced the two contradictory settings together: Boston and the Cape in one.

Luckily, we all have our suitcases with us, since we're leaving behind the hostel life and heading to a hotel tonight. There's a large changing area connected to a beach bar, and I'm definitely tempted to get a coffee. We go straight for the restrooms, and thank goodness the place is clean. Pristine white stalls and curtained changing rooms—I feel like someone must have just tidied up in here. The only exception is the sand, dusted over the concrete floor.

I change back into my cutout one-piece because who knew we were going to have so much swimming time in late December?

Saron and I walk out together and put down our towels about halfway between the beach bar and the water. Before she lays down, Saron spots Jess.

"Hey, come join us," Saron says, waving Jess over. "We've bonded now; you don't have a choice."

Which is why Jess is lying next to me on one side, Saron on the other. Jess has her new floppy hat covering her face, and I think she might be napping.

Saron is propped up, her gaze set on Etan, one of the new Israelis. He's sitting on a towel a little ahead of us, and I think he might be flexing. "I wouldn't mind licking that," she says under her breath. Then she turns to me. "Do you see this?"

I think she must still be talking about Etan and his muscles, but then she nods to Sammy and Max.

The two of them are swimming. Max is floating, and Sammy keeps nudging him, making him move through the water. I kind of want to join them, but I also don't want to get in the way. They look so cute, playing around like that. So I'm lying in the sun (aka praying I don't burn up like a vampire exposed to daylight) and doing some reading. My trusty hat is on my head and my water bottle is by my side.

After a couple of chapters, David comes jogging over. He's wearing a pair of pale-blue swim trunks and a plain white T-shirt. "Jess, you're on bag duty," he says.

Jess just groans, which makes me think she's definitely asleep.

"We agreed on turns, and Batya can't watch them all by herself."

Jess groans again, but this time she gets up. She flips David off as she walks away. I can see why Saron thought it was okay to bring her into our little scheme.

David sits down in her spot. "So, ladies, how's the beach treating you both? I feel like I haven't touched base with you two all morning."

"Can you take your flirting elsewhere? I'm working," Saron says.

Wow, okay, why did she say that? He definitely wasn't flirting. He was innocently asking us how we were doing and it was directed at both of us and you can't flirt with two people at the same time, can you?

Apparently, David is not freaking out about the comment. He simply asks, "Working?"

I look over at Saron. She's lying on her belly, head toward the water, her sketch pad at the edge of her towel. She pushes it a little so that we can see what's on the page.

She's working on a new dress. This one has a high neckline and long sleeves. The top has a cityscape design, rows of tightly packed buildings along the chest that extend to the neck and sleeves. It abruptly stops at an empire waist, a line of tan next to which Saron has written: *ribbon?* The skirt is a blend of three different shades of blue.

"It's a commentary on the suffocating nature of humanity. We take up the available land, essentially overcrowding the space we have, but the majority of the Earth is covered in water. It's a representation of the land and the ocean, inspired by this beach. Loosely. Does that make sense?"

"Of course," I say. I don't know much about fashion, but I do know how to boost a creative ego.

"My only worry is that I'm trying to connect my designs to this trip. Not just based off the inspiration. It needs something more. Something specific to Israel. I mean, I could technically use this one to talk about somewhere like the Chicago Lakefront, you know? My cousins live there. It's the same thing, the beaches right next to the city." She pauses, looking at her own sketch like it might start talking to her.

"You could try engaging with the beach," David offers. "See if there's something Israel-specific in the experience."

"I'll take that into consideration," she says. She keeps her eyes on the page in front of her, giving no sign that she's going to move anytime soon.

David laughs and then turns to me. "Want to swim?" Without waiting for my answer, he gets up and takes off his T-shirt.

I shouldn't stare at David. That's gross and creepy. I shouldn't stare at another person, basically objectifying them, even if their arms really are toned and they look like a super-tall, athletic model god without their shirt on.

"You coming?" he asks.

"Yeah, I'd love to water," I say. "I'd love to go in the water," I try again.

That went well. Gold star.

I get up and follow him.

I do love the water. Love love it. My family grew up going to the Cape, and I basically spent every non-camp week floating in the Atlantic with Cat. I step into the water, prepared for the usual submerged-in-ice reaction, but the temperature is so nice. I'm basically standing in a giant spa bathtub. Honestly, it feels warmer here than it was lying on the beach.

I wade in deeper until the water is up to my belly. No rush of cold, just the calm, still ocean. I take a deep breath.

David looks right at me. Then he splashes.

"How old are you again?" I ask, wiping water from my eyes. It's super salty in a painful, stinging way.

"On my birthday, I'll be four."

I splash him back.

"Ow, wait, I forgot how salty it is here. I take it all back."

"The splash has already been sploshed," I say, voice jokingly serious.

"Sploshed?" he questions.

I nod.

"Now, are there any other completely absurd and made-up words you would like to submit for consideration to the dictionary subcommittee or should we just stick to the ones we already have?"

"Dictionary subcommittee?" I ask. "Which you are a part of?"

"Naturally," he says.

"Oh, no, please continue. I would love to know more about this mysterious subcommittee. Which dictionary is it exactly that you're affiliated with? How do you feel about these young'uns and their interwebs speak? What are your thoughts on 'yeet'?"

David places a hand on his chin, as though he is deeply considering his responses for each question. "Well," he begins, "the answer to each one of those questions can really be summed up by—" He splashes me again.

Meaning we are in an all-out splash war by the time Max swims over, holding Sammy in his arms. "We're playing a game. We need another team."

I raise an eyebrow.

"It's a dunking game," he continues. "So one partner picks up the other, like this. The holder asks questions, and the one being held has five seconds to answer them or they get dunked. Two teams, answering questions at the same time. First team who has to dunk loses."

"If we're competing against you, couldn't we just ignore the dunk rule and win?"

"Wow, okay, dirty cheater," Max says. He lets Sammy go so they can both stand up to talk to us.

"I'm just saying, it really doesn't sound like you playtested this."

"We could get a ref," Sammy offers.

Max looks around. Saron and our banner friends are lying out on the beach, so it looks like Max is going to have to choose someone new. Which feels weird.

The old Max could do that. He had this magic ability to reach out to strangers and walk away with a new friend. Now he's admitted to me that it's tough for him. I should be the one to find someone; he shouldn't have that pressure.

I don't get the chance to even offer my help. "Amit seems cool," Max says. He turns around and starts wading through the water. "Amit, we've got a job for you," he calls out.

Watching him feels like progress.

Max explains the rules to Amit, the only one of the Israelis to brave the water, in an exchange that involves some gesturing and a lot of repeated phrases because Amit is hella confused about what this weird American is trying to get him to do.

"Does an obsession with games run in your family?" David asks.

"Genetic predisposition," I say.

We're sort of staring at each other, and I'm starting to get a little worried about the thought of David touching me. Not that, well . . . I should be into it. Aren't people supposed to want to be touched? But touching in general has always made me super uncomfortable.

Max comes splashing back. "Amit's in."

So now I'm in a boy's arms in the Mediterranean Sea, and I can feel him holding the crooks of my legs, his arms around my shoulders, and all I can think of is the fact that this is a strange person. Touching my body. We barely know each other and sure, we've been friendly and he seems nice, but does that even mean anything? His body is on my body.

I don't like it and I think I'm supposed to like it and I don't know how I feel about the fact that I don't like it.

I start to think about the whole thing as though it's happening to someone else, some normal girl who is fine with some normal boy holding her in the water in a pretty platonic context. This normal girl doesn't even care that she's known this normal boy for only a few days because they've bonded, and that means something. It should mean something, right?

Max's voice pulls me out of my head. "Amit's asking the questions; I've told him to go hard on us. Then he asked what that meant, so I compared it to Never Have I Ever and he asked what that was, but we're good to go now. Since he's asking, we're going to take turns holding each other, since the water basically does most of the holding anyway. So two teams, answering the same question at the same time, but now we are taking turns answering questions within our teams. Everyone got it?"

It's important to note that Amit still looks pretty lost.

"Amit, ask the first question," Max prompts. He's already holding Sammy in the water, primed to dunk if necessary.

"All right, eh, you do the drugs?" Amit asks.

"Never, not my thing," I say quickly. "Switch."

I can't really hear Sammy's answer because of a combination of adrenaline and a compulsory need to win. I move to stand up and take David loosely in my arms as fast as I can because the game pressure is on but now I'm sort of holding him (though the water is really doing most of the work) and that is not better; why am I like this?

"What is, eh, sex thing you like?" Amit asks.

"Kind of always wanted a girl to cook for me wearing nothing but an apron," David says, equally rushed. "Switch!"

That makes it worse because now there's this sexual edge to it and a weirdly specific one at that, and I need to stop thinking about all of this because we are in the middle of a game.

"Do you go . . . naked swimming?"

"Okay, actually yes, but it was with my best friend and we did it to say that we had skinny-dipped. Switch!"

"Eh, now, how much people have you sex with?" Amit asks.

"Two. Ex-girlfriend, sorta serious and then fizzled out, and a one-night stand; turns out that is not my thing. Switch."

This was weird before, but now I know he has slept with two girls . . . and I have never slept with anyone or kissed anyone or held anyone's hand in a romantic not *buddies on an elementary school field trip* way. And this is probably the most Boy Contact I have ever had and I don't even think I like it but he has had Girl Contact with two different people and why do I think this way; why won't my brain just shut the eff up?

I'm still thinking all these things when Amit says, "Do you like a person now?" and honestly, how do I respond to that, because I thought maybe David might be a potential romantic prospect, like if I were the one who needed one, which I don't, but even if I wanted to, I apparently don't even really like him because I'm super uncomfortable with his body touching my body even though this is obviously not romantic touching, and then I think about the possibility of him romantically touching me like he has touched not one but two other girls and it makes me feel kind of sick but I've thought about sex with another person before, like in the abstract, and I do like scenes in movies where the romantic leads finally make out or get it on after all that buildup, but I'm not in a movie and I will never be in a movie—

And that's about when I get dunked in the water.

WAY DOWN HADESTOWN

We drive to Mount Herzl, the national cemetery. It seems weird to go right from the beach to here, but apparently it was the only time that fit with the schedule.

I sit quietly next to Saron on the bus. I can't stop thinking about the beach. She's still focused on her sketch, and I wonder if I should interrupt her work to confide in her.

No, definitely not; she'll laugh at me for being some weird prude who panics over touch. Who is still panicking, for some pathetic reason, even though the moment is over.

When we pull up to the cemetery, I stop myself. I can't keep thinking like this. Not here.

The first thing I notice is that it looks like a carefully curated garden, neat and organized and green. This is a place that is meant to be visited, lush with flowers lining the headstones.

We see the resting places of political figures and military

leaders. These are different from the other graves, slick black monuments with Hebrew writing. The rest are lighter in color, raised stone around a bed of greenery, some plants, some flowers. All beginning with a white stone, featuring epitaphs written in Hebrew. So different in the appearances of their planters, so similar in their continued care.

We stop in a newer area where there are fewer headstones. Rivkah walks forward.

"This"—she points to a grave, right in the middle of the second row—"is my brother.

"He was in the IDF for five years; he was a brave soldier. But he found his death when there were bombings in our village, when he was home. They let him be buried here." She takes a polished stone out of her pocket and places it on the headstone. "Thank you for listening."

Shira walks over and pats her arm. She whispers in Rivkah's ear. Rivkah nods. She says something quietly back in Hebrew.

I feel like I shouldn't be watching.

I walk away. Max follows.

I sit down on a patch of grass, so open after the lines of headstones. I realize that this is the space for the people who haven't died yet. Someday there will be headstones here too.

"Her brother died," I say, looking up at Max.

"I know." Max sits down next to me.

"Her brother," I repeat.

Max reaches over and squeezes my arm.

"I really thought . . . when I got the call that night, I

thought you might not . . ." I don't know how to get the words out.

"I'm right here," he says.

I nod. "I can't lose you. I don't know how to *be* without you."

He doesn't say anything in response. What could he say? He can't promise that he'll always be with me; he can't promise that he'll always be safe. Those aren't guarantees.

We sit there together for a few minutes, looking over the graves.

Max breaks the silence. "I haven't been to a cemetery since—"

"We don't need to talk about it," I cut him off.

"Okay," Max says. "If you change your mind, I'm here."

Our group visits one more grave. An American boy who made aliyah, immigrating to Israel. A boy who was young and who died in the Israeli Defense Forces. And instead of just rocks on the headstone, there's a display of tour group name tags and old hats and water bottles and signs and letters, completely covering the raised flower bed. A full memorial that blankets a single grave.

The sun is starting to set over the cemetery, the sky painted orange and peach and pink. *It's beautiful*, I think, as we head to the bus.

FAMILY

"Tah-lee, Mohx," Uncle Ezzie croons, walking toward us through the hotel lobby.

Ezra is technically our great-uncle, though he looks way too young for that. There's a twelve-year age gap between Safta and Uncle Ezzie, so he basically grew up with her like another mom. He walks through the lobby like everyone has been waiting for him. I think about main character entrances in opening scenes—the start of a play, the first song in a musical. He is ready to sing.

"You grew!" he exclaims, eyeing the two of us. "Too big! I held you as babies."

"I think you shrunk a little," Max responds.

"Aha, yes, you noticed!" he says as though he has been working very hard at getting older. "Now, I take you; we eat, we discuss dark family history. Good times!"

Max and I follow him out of the hotel.

I wasn't sure if we were going to get to see Uncle Ezzie, since our trip schedule has been so packed, but then Chaya announced that we had some free time to explore Tel Aviv after our nightly debrief. Which was perfect because he lives on the outskirts of the city.

He walks us to his car. He's parked in a small alleyway off our hotel.

"We're not really allowed to go all that far," I say, standing by the car door. When Chaya told us we could go out, she also gave us very strict boundaries and an even stricter curfew.

Max looks at me like I just told a teacher they forgot to give homework.

"Nonsense! You are with family. These things do not matter." Uncle Ezzie waves toward the car. "We go, we are safe, you return in one piece."

The drive isn't all that long, maybe fifteen minutes? I watch through the window as we drive out of the city, buildings now giving one another some space to breathe. I think the road might be wider now.

We pull up in front of an apartment building. "This is it!" Uncle Ezzie exclaims.

"Your house?" Max asks.

"No, no, better. This is where your safta and I grew up."

We're in front of a three-story building on the outskirts of Tel Aviv. It looks like all the other buildings lining the street: squat and tan, like they've been crafted out of sand.

I picture Safta outside, her blond curls tousled over her

face as she does a handstand by those steps or walks around holding baby Ezzie like her very own doll. In my mind, her face is frozen, crafted from the family photos she keeps in haphazardly organized albums.

By the time she was my age, she was in the IDF. In a year, she would be leaving home and moving to a new country. This was the place she had to leave behind.

"Let's call your safta," Uncle Ezzie says, pulling me back to the present. "She will like that we are here." He takes out his phone and dials. "Alma, dear, I'm with the kids. Wait. Yes, they look healthy. I'll put you on the speaker."

"Hi, Safta!" I say.

"Hey, Safta."

"Motekim, oh my heart is just bursting from your voices."

"We love you too, Saftale," I say.

"Oh, bubbeleh, is it everything you wished?"

"We're having lots of fun," Max says.

"We went rafting, and we've seen Jaffa and Tel Aviv. We're going to Jerusalem later," I add.

"Alma, Alma. I was showing the kids where we grew up," Uncle Ezzie says.

"Oh, well! I do not know the last time I was there. Kids, our sabba used to have a clinic in that house. He was known. A dentist. And our safta. A rebel! Very left," she says.

I have no concept of what *very left* means in this context. Safta has talked a little about her family and what it was like growing up here. I know they were here at the time of the British Mandate. I remember her telling me about the

British soldiers, how they had set up a curfew and would stop people and ask questions, usually without prompting. She told me that they scared her, that she grew up with fear. Does this mean her grandma was somehow fighting against them? Working with some top secret Israeli group? To do what?

Before I can ask any questions, Safta continues.

"It is important to think back." She pauses. "What will you kids do tomorrow?"

"We're going to Yad Vashem," Max explains. The Holocaust Museum.

"Oh, dark days, but we must remember," says Safta. "On my mother's side, we are Polish. The family, the ones who stayed, they were sent to Treblinka. That was the camp. Treblinka."

She pauses again.

I feel like my chest is too tight right now. I knew that we had family who died in the Holocaust, but hearing the name of the concentration camp they were sent to makes it feel more concrete.

Safta's voice shifts, lighter now. "Oh, I just send you so much love! You two have the best time. Best. Oh, I wish I was with you. How I wish!" she says. "I don't want to keep you. Tell me all after. Mwah-mwah."

"Send our love to Sabba," I say.

"Yes, of course, katshkelah," she says. "Little duckling," her special name for me. "Ezra, you show them a good time."

After Uncle Ezzie hangs up, he drives us to his home.

"It's not much," he says as he parks in front of a one-story beige house.

I picture the Colonial homes in our town, all decked out with lights for the holidays. Of course that wouldn't be the same here; Hanukkah isn't even an important event, traditionally speaking. Back home, it's amped up to compete with Christmas, but that doesn't matter in Israel.

There are no lights here—not draped around the squared, industrial structure or hanging from the flat roof, not even left on inside.

Uncle Ezzie opens the front door and flips on the switch.

I expect the interior to look old, like something out of a museum, but it's modern and sleek, with sharp edges and simple designs. There are chic, plastic black chairs set around a metal table and gray armchairs that look like they're meant to be looked at rather than used.

I notice two framed photos on either side of the door, enlarged and set against painted black wood and glass. One is of Uncle Ezzie and his daughters when they were little, the color faded. Uncle Ezzie has significantly more hair and a thick mustache in the photo, which seems weird, since I've always known him clean-shaven and balding. The other is a black-and-white photograph of a girl holding hands with a little boy, who looks just old enough to stand, in front of two adults.

"Is that . . . ?" I start, nodding to the photo.

Uncle Ezzie nods. "Your great-grandparents. That is Shmuel and that is Alina."

I know I met both of them before they died because I've seen the pictures of Great-Grandma Alina reading to us as babies and Great-Grandpa Shmuel sitting between us at our first Passover, Max and me in high chairs on either side. I don't remember them, though, not really. And definitely not like this, standing behind their young children in stiff, formal clothing.

"Now, I had an idea," Uncle Ezzie starts, walking over to the kitchen, just past the metal dining table. "How would you feel making some family dishes?"

"That sounds great," Max says.

We follow Uncle Ezzie. The kitchen has a long gray counter with a deep porcelain sink, completely empty, and a tall, thin refrigerator that looks brand-new.

Uncle Ezzie unloads the ingredients for three dishes onto the smooth concrete counter. We're making an Israeli salad, chicken schnitzel, and cottage-cheese pancakes. Uncle Ezzie puts Max in charge of dicing the tomatoes, cucumbers, and radishes for the salad while the two of us prepare the breading for the chicken.

"When we were young, there was not much," Uncle Ezzie says. "The pancakes, those are a way to take the leftover flour and egg from the schnitzel, so we don't waste. Your great-grandmother, she would only season with salt and pepper," he adds. "We have more. Each generation, you take the recipe and you change for what you have. If you are the one cooking, you are allowed to change." He adds cumin, paprika, and garlic powder to the bowls with the flour, eggs, and bread crumbs.

The room is filled with the thick stench of fried oil. It smells like when I make latkes for Hanukkah.

Dad never cooks like this. He's more likely to make chicken parm than chicken schnitzel. Even when I make latkes, Mom is the one who helps me shred the potatoes and the onions. I guess I've seen him eat matzah around Passover, but putting some butter on a glorified cracker doesn't really count.

Does he remember these dishes? He must have had them before; he used to visit his grandparents here in Israel every summer when he was growing up.

I watch Uncle Ezzie carefully as he cooks so I can try to re-create it at home. Maybe Dad can help.

We catch up as we cook. Uncle Ezzie tells us stories about his daughters, who we haven't seen since we were little, as he pounds the chicken breast into thin slices. He talks about our safta growing up while mixing the cottage cheese in with the rest of the eggs and flour. As we set the table, he reminisces about the coffeehouse their father owned and explains how our great-grandmother studied microbiology in a time before women were guaranteed an education.

We talk too. Max and I tell Uncle Ezzie all about our family and our lives as we sit down to eat our great-grandmother's dishes. Part of it feels silly and generic, like we are running through everything that has happened since the last time we saw him, but he seems genuinely interested in the minutiae of American high school extracurriculars and whether or not our parents are in good health.

I take a bite of the chicken schnitzel as Max starts to talk about how Mom and Dad are doing at work. I don't know what to expect; we usually don't cook with these seasonings at home. The breading has an earthy, warm taste with a slight kick. It's absolutely delicious.

I'm on my second piece when Uncle Ezzie asks Max, "How are you feeling, after the accident?"

I stop chewing.

"Well, I have a cool new scar," Max says, raising his left eyebrow.

Uncle Ezzie stays silent.

"I was really lucky," Max continues hesitantly. "That everything healed and I was able to get medical leave for the beginning of school. I was a little worried about getting a good start to the year, because colleges still care about grades and everything for the first semester of senior year."

I frown. He's acting like he's cared about school this whole time. Is he just trying to make it seem like everything is okay in front of Uncle Ezzie?

Before I can say anything, Uncle Ezzie exclaims, "Colleges! Oh, the excitement. Where are you kids applying?"

"Boston University," I say. "I got in early decision. Max is going to apply there for the regular decision deadline."

"I haven't decided where I'm going yet," Max says, voice dismissive. Like this hasn't been in the works for years. Like this wasn't always a part of our plan.

"I also applied to Berklee College of Music and some schools out of state," he continues. "Carnegie Mellon, Oberlin,

U of M Ann Arbor. I even applied to Trinity, in Dublin, which is a long shot, but . . ."

This must be a mistake. He hasn't applied to college yet. That's why we're here, in Israel. That's why I've been busting my butt for the last three days. "You applied to all those schools already?" I ask quietly.

"Yeah, what did you think I'd do? Miss the deadlines?"

I grab my napkin and squeeze it under the table. *Yes*, I thought he was going to miss the deadlines. Of course I thought that. He didn't apply early with me; he never talked about schools. He was being antisocial and completely wasting his senior year. He had given up.

What else was I going to think?

"I thought we'd already figured out college," I say, voice shaking.

Max doesn't respond.

Uncle Ezzie clears his throat. "More salad?" he asks, picking up the bowl.

I grab the bowl a little too aggressively, spilling some of the salad on the table. *Perfect.*

I can't stop thinking about Max for the rest of dinner. He applied to schools already? When? At first I think he must have done it today, because it wouldn't make sense for him to do it before. He was sobbing in his room last night. I saw him. He was still depressed, and depressed Max wouldn't apply to school. He didn't when we were supposed to back in November. He must have done it right before dinner.

I know logically that can't be true. We've been so busy on

the trip and, if he really did apply to all those schools, he would have needed time.

He must have applied before we left and didn't tell me.

I should be happy. He applied; that's all that should matter. But it doesn't.

And to be honest, I'm not sure why that is.

Max and I volunteer to wash all the dishes while Uncle Ezzie looks for some old family photographs to show us before he drives us back to the hotel. I wait until he is in the other room, then pounce.

"What the hell?" I say, putting down the stack of dishes next to the sink.

Max turns on the faucet. "Care to elaborate?"

"You applied to schools, and you didn't tell me."

"What are you, my keeper?"

I clench my fists so tightly that I can feel my fidget ring pressing into my other fingers. "You should have said something," I say.

"Why, so you could apply to those schools too?" he asks, handing me a wet plate. "You're already going to BU."

I grab a dish towel and start to dry the plate. "You know what I mean. You didn't say anything, you didn't apply with me, and then all of a sudden you want to go far away and spend a fortune on school? Trinity? Really?"

"So now I'm not allowed to make any decisions without you?" He starts scrubbing the fried-chicken pan.

I watch him for a second, scrubbing like nothing is wrong. "Stop it, Max! Just stop. I can't believe you've convinced yourself that you can go that far after everything that's happened. You can barely leave the house!"

"Don't turn this on me," he says.

"What's that supposed to mean?" I ask, trying to keep my voice quiet enough so Uncle Ezzie won't hear. "You know, you've been a mess ever since the accident. Ever since the driver—"

"*Driver?* Seriously, Tally? You can't even say her name?" He drops the sponge in the sink and turns to stare at me. "That *driver* was your best friend, Tally. *Cat.* She was your best friend."

I jerk back.

No. No, she wasn't. Best friends wouldn't do what she did. Best friends don't hurt you like this. Best friends don't break promises. Best friends don't put your brother in danger. Best friends don't drive drunk and crash their parents' car into a telephone pole.

Best friends don't die at seventeen.

"I can't believe you," Max says. "You won't talk about her. You won't mourn. Cat died, Tal. She's gone. Cat, who we grew up with. Cat, who planned out our whole lives together. Cat, who spent every goddamn Friday night sleeping in your room when we were in middle school—"

I shake my head. "Shut up, shut up. Just stop."

"No, Tally! You keep making me feel like I'm some delicate flower, just because I'm grieving. But you won't even admit that you're affected by any of this. It's like you can't mourn." He shakes his head. "You know what? I'm done. I don't need this right now."

He walks out of the kitchen, leaving me with the rest of the dishes.

My whole body feels numb.

I step over to the sink and turn on the water. I start to scrub the salad bowl. If all I think about is cleaning, then I don't have to think about Max or anything he said. I can keep scrubbing, possibly forever, until all I hear is the loud, rushing water coming out of the faucet and nothing else.

The bowl slips out of my hands and cracks.

I pretend I'm upset about the bowl.

SHE USED TO BE MINE

I hear Max's voice on repeat the whole ride to the hotel. *She was your best friend. She was your best friend.*

Was was was.

I walk right to my room. Saron and Sammy are my roommates for the night, but they're nowhere to be seen. They must still be out. I grab my phone, sitting at the edge of my bed, and look at my message from Cat.

Cat: THIS BETTER BE INSPIRING YOU! YOU OWE ME SONGS. still not talking to you kay love you hun

Everything is fine. Everything is fine. She's—

She's gone, Tal, Max said, that night in the back of the ambulance.

Except it didn't make sense, because they were at a stupid cast party, just some people from drama club getting together to sit around in a basement. Completely unimportant. Which was why I stayed behind.

This better be inspiring you!

I didn't write anything back. The last thing she ever texted me and I didn't even respond to her.

It wasn't the last thing she said to me, though. No, that was a couple of hours later, my phone vibrating on my nightstand.

A call. She rarely called, unless she was too lazy or too tired. Maybe that should have tipped me off.

"Hun," she started, voice raspy over the phone. "Your brother is drunk."

"Oy vey," I said. I remember being distracted by the muffled noise of voices in the background because I hadn't turned off the TV.

"Don't worry, I'll basically be a superhero and bring him home," she said. "I can fix any problem."

I laughed. "You're just coming over because you want to watch more *High School Musical: The Musical: The Series*," I said. "I got you all figured out."

"Hmm, do you?" Her voice was exaggerated, silly, but I didn't realize. I thought we were just joking around. "Don't know what you could possibly mean because I'm currently not talking to you."

"Uh-huh."

"But if the show happens to be on . . ."

"All figured out."

I could picture her response. She was probably shaking

her head, her nose crinkled despite her best efforts, like it always did when she was amused. Out loud, she said, "Be there soon!"

That was it. I played it in my head on a loop those first few weeks without her. I pictured her crinkled nose, her smile, and her flushed cheeks so clearly that I almost convinced myself that I was there. I heard her words so loud and so suffocating that I knew I had to stop.

Be there soon!

She was wrong. She never reached my house. She never dropped Max off. She never finished the show with me. She never applied to Boston College. She won't be there at senior prom. She won't graduate. She won't move into an apartment with me for our junior year of college. She won't help me pick out a wedding dress or be my maid of honor. She won't be my future kids' godmother. She won't be.

I miss Cat so much that it's like a physical part of me has been ripped away. I miss our past. I miss her potential. I miss every silly tradition we built up since we were in elementary school. I miss the way her hair always smelled like apples and cinnamon. I miss falling asleep during a movie with my head on her shoulder. I miss our sleepovers, talking to her late at night, when we were supposed to be asleep. The time of night when there were no secrets.

I miss feeling like I knew her.

Because I didn't know that body, cracked and bloody and lifeless, as it was taken out of the totaled car. I didn't know she would drive drunk. I didn't know. I was supposed to know.

It was easier to put out of my mind. It was easier to blame some faceless friend of Max's for the car crash, for being so reckless, for being gone, and keep my Cat alive. It was easier to lock the truth somewhere so deep inside me that I hoped it might never escape.

It has escaped.

I guess I'm crying. I guess that's what's happening with my body. But I am not there. I'm not there. She's not here.

She's not here to help me with my panic attacks. She's not here to make tea and remind me to breathe and to practice the meditation techniques she researched.

She used to be there for me. Why wasn't I there for her?

If I had gone to that party, maybe she would still be alive. But no, I told her I wanted to watch that stupid movie instead. That we could hang out after.

There was no after.

Maybe I could have stopped her. But what would I have done? I can't drive. I guess we could have walked. I could have called our parents. Should I have? I talked to her. I knew there was alcohol; she told me Max was drunk. She didn't tell me that she had been drinking. Should I have known anyway? She told me she was going to drive. I didn't know she would drive drunk. I should have known. I should have stopped it.

It hurts like I'm hollow. Like there's nothing left inside. No spirit, no air. Nothing. I am nothing without her.

I put down my phone on the nightstand by the bed. I get

up, turn off the lights in the room, and climb under the covers still in my clothes from the day.

Max was right.

I am the one who is broken. I am the one who is selfish. I am the one who couldn't save her best friend.

WORDS FAIL

The mood is pretty somber on the bus ride to Yad Vashem. Which makes sense.

I look over at Max, sitting near the front of the bus. We've been avoiding each other all morning.

I don't want to talk to him. I don't want to deal with his judgment. I don't want to hear him yell at me to mourn.

I don't want to mourn.

We pull up to the museum, still quiet. It's too bright outside for how dim I feel.

When Max and I were little, we went to the Holocaust Museum in DC. It was part of this big road trip, and we were sort of already emotionally worn down from being forced to coexist in a car together for ages, but Mom insisted.

There are two things I remember from the trip. The first was the kids' section. We were twelve, which made us just old enough to think we did not qualify as kids. We walked through the whole exhibit. They have you follow a little boy's life and see how he gets moved to the ghetto and later to a concentration camp. How his identity is stripped away, his family murdered, his life lost.

The second thing I remember was the hair, piled behind glass cases.

I don't know if I can go through that again, especially now. That probably makes me a selfish monster. My problems are nothing compared to mass-scale murder. I just can't help thinking that it would be easier if we made this stop at a different time. Tomorrow, at least.

My life is so little compared to all this. I think about how Safta said it's important to remember. *It is.*

It's important to contextualize these horrific events because they didn't happen to people who existed in the generic long-ago time but to real people, really recently. There are people still alive today who lived through it. That's not going to be true soon, and that scares me because it's too easy to designate events to the past tense and forget.

And repeat.

I keep thinking about my family. The great-great relatives who were stripped and shaved and tattooed and starved and gassed and burned. Treblinka. That's where they were sent. I have the name now.

How can that have happened in a time with cars and phones and medicine? How are we still allowing people to be murdered based on who they are or where they were born? Why don't we as a people ever learn our lesson?

We've got a new guide, one who works at the museum. She hands out headphones and these little radios so we can all hear her during the tour. "I want you to know, this is about respect. We are respecting the lives. We are remembering. If you need to take a moment, please do. We respect and remember in our own ways."

When we first walk in, there's a video playing that takes up a whole wall. Different films stitched together, a line of men doing the hora, two little girls waving. Just people, doing everyday things. Just people, living.

These people's lives are about to be utterly ruined, and they have no idea. I think maybe this is supposed to remind us that times weren't always bad, but all I can think is that they don't know. They don't know that the lives they have crafted, their hopes and dreams and plans, are about to become irrelevant. Everything is going to be about hatred and survival, and most of them aren't going to survive.

They don't know. They don't know how bad it will get. They don't know those might be their happiest memories. They don't know. They didn't know. I didn't know.

I shake my head. I'm not going to think about her now. This place is bigger than what's going on in my life.

We walk farther into the museum. The rooms are arranged so that visitors walk through the history, events ordered chronologically so that we see propaganda turn into violence. Businesses destroyed, Stars of David stitched onto clothes. People rounded up, told to dig their own graves, and murdered.

I take out my headphones and walk ahead. I need to get away from the group.

I find a room filled with art. Even in the ghettos, there was art. Secret paintings and music and hand-sewn dolls. I wonder, if I lived then, would I have had enough in me to create? Could I have stood there, a gold star on my coat, and sung?

The group has passed me now, but I can see them ahead. I refuse to read the signs, even though there are English translations, because I already know what they're going to say. At the end of the room, there's a model of a gas chamber, tiny figurine people crowded and starved and dying. I realize the group has stopped in front of a glass panel in the floor, just before the model. I walk over and look down and see the shoes.

Their shoes.

I put my headphones back in.

". . . and they told her, you are the one. You will be blessed. They told her on the train, and when they got off, they were sent in one direction. She was sent in the other. She knew later they were killed.

"She was in the camp when she was told they were moving to a new place. First they would need to be clean. It was the hope. Why hope when you know the smell? Why hope when people do not return? They were naked, hundreds of women, and they were happy. They were going to be clean; this had not happened since the arrival. They pushed; they wanted it to be true.

"She did not push. She remembered the words of her family.

"It was then that people noticed. Packed in a room, no soap or towels. They faced the lie.

"Then the door opened. They had made a mistake; they did not need to kill as many, so they took the women in back. The rest had the gas.

"I talked to her years ago. She was old, but she still remembered. She remembered G-d. I ask why, why were there lies, why was there hope? She said everything then was about lies. But the hope, she said, without the hope, there would be no end. There would be no survivor. There would be no more of the story."

I look at the shoes again, piled together. The story did not end. We are here and we remember. We are the blood of the bloodshed. I can walk down the street without a star stitched to my clothes, and I can go to temple, and I can sit at a Jewish deli. I've always been physically safe. It's not like I've been profiled walking down the street. I have that privilege, the privilege of being safe, that used to be a mere dream.

When we leave the museum building, we see our first view of Jerusalem, the whole city stretched out before us. While the museum felt almost industrial, gray with concrete slabs cutting through the exhibit rooms, this feels so much lighter. There's greenery around us, trees and bushes, and farther out, there are buildings of white and tan and brown. There are people walking around, living their lives. It's complicated and it's messy and it's full of life.

I think we're going to leave, but the guide tells us there's one more thing we need to see.

"When you enter, Children's Memorial is dark. Hold on to the railing."

It's a slow procession, all of us in line, hands against the metal rail on the wall. At first there's nothing but that darkness, but then I turn the corner. It looks like we are in a room of captured stars, stretching back forever. It takes me a moment to realize that they aren't stars. They're candles, tiny flames that burn as bright as the lights that were snuffed out.

There's a recorded track over the speaker. It's simple, just the names and ages of the children killed.

Children. They killed the children. I knew that—of course I knew that—and I don't know why it feels worse than hearing the other stories because those are horrific. But children need us. They *need* us. They can't survive by themselves. They did not have a say and they did not have a chance and they did not grow.

I wish that we had ended on hope. I try to remember that hope. I try to remember that I'm safe, but it's hard to feel that way when you see the lights of murdered children stretching on and on and on.

I think about a phrase Safta taught me. Le'olam lo. Not in this world, never again. We can never let this happen again. We will never let this happen again. There's a point when you need to say that children should not be murdered. There's a point when you need to take action to make sure that they are safe. Be it from Nazis, be it from white supremacists, be it from government officials, be it from lunatics with guns. Be it from people you thought were safe, who can end up being the most dangerous of them all. Le'olam lo.

Never again.

≡ ——— ≈

This day needs to be over.

When we get back to the hotel, Chaya has one more thing she wants us to do. She sits us down in a conference room.

"Today was tough, I know. So why do we do this? On a tour of Israel, why do we need this day?

"This is a part of us and of our histories. As Jewish people, we are told to remember. To honor.

"So I want a space for us. I want to hear your stories. I want you to honor and remember the personal things that you have been through. This is a time for the processing."

It's quiet for a while. Then Joshua raises his hand. "When I was in elementary school, kids used to throw pennies at me. Called me a greedy Jew." He looks at the floor.

Gabriel claps him on the back. "Same thing happened to me, with the pennies." He pauses. "There were other things too. One time, I was at this work party for my mom, and one of her colleagues asked me if I knew Drake because he's also Black and Jewish."

A girl raises her hand, Yael I think? "I've been told I'm not a real Jew because I don't look like one. What does that even mean? I don't look like a Jew. Are we all supposed to be clones?"

"Oh, well," Sammy starts without raising her hand. "This girl from my high school once asked me if my daddy was going to pay for a new nose when I turned sixteen. I asked her what the hell she was talking about and she was all like, *No, I heard that you JAPs always get new noses*, and then she said I should be happy that I have enough money for it." She folds her arms over her chest and slumps down in her chair.

I think about the propaganda at Yad Vashem, depictions of Jewish people with large, crooked noses, hoarding money. I can't believe Sammy went through that.

I've never faced such blatant antisemitism. The worst comments I've heard about being Jewish are when people say things like, "I've never met a Jew before," or, "You're not like other Jews," and then basically look at me as a spokesperson for a whole group of people who are Other.

Jess raises her hand. Chaya looks over at her, head tilted like she's surprised, but then nods.

"You know, I've been through it too," Jess says. "I was at a party, and this girl asked me to help her get some cookies out of the oven. Then she said, 'You're Jewish, right? Your people are *real* comfortable with ovens,' and started laughing." Jess huffs. "Holocaust jokes, great way to lighten up a party."

I don't understand how anyone could think that is an acceptable joke.

I think about the picture of my great-grandparents that was hanging by Uncle Ezzie's door. My great-grandma lost her family in the Holocaust. *Treblinka*, I think. I wonder if she ever found out how they died. Did they get sick? Were they sent to the gas chambers? I feel nauseous even thinking about that.

I feel this layer of guilt too. My great-grandparents survived; my family survived. I'm safe.

I shouldn't feel guilty for being safe, but I do. I didn't experience the terrible things that they did, so I shouldn't claim their trauma as my own.

Being Jewish isn't even something that defines my whole life. I mean, I was raised interfaith. A lot of people don't even know that my dad's whole side of the family is Jewish. Some people don't even think that counts.

I raise my hand. "I've been told I'm not a real Jew 'cause my dad is the one who's Jewish. Which is just ridiculous; I mean, my grandma, my safta, is Israeli. That whole side of the family is Jewish." I pause. "You know I found out last night which camp our relatives were sent to? Treblinka. If we were alive then . . . All you needed was one grandparent who was Jewish. That was it; that was all you needed to be killed."

Eli, one of the Israelis, speaks without raising his hand. "They're right, though. You are not Jewish; it must be on the mother's side."

I close my eyes. I can feel my nails digging into my left hand.

Chaya stops him. "That is the Orthodox view. When Roman invaders a long time ago raped Jewish women, there was a decision that only the mother needs to be Jewish. It was to continue the line. That is why they say the mother must be Jewish."

This is not technically true, or at least the truth is more complicated. I've heard my mom talk about this before. She's told me about how Orthodox and Conservative Jews have different views on the reason it is believed that the mother must be Jewish. Some point to spiritual reasons; some note that biblical men married women who were not Jewish, so the custom had to change. Reform Jews don't typically care all that much to begin with.

Really, they just didn't want you to intermarry anyone, Mom told me. *Oops.*

I guess the problem is that when I hear people say that it has to be on your mother's side, what I really hear is that I don't count. That half of my family doesn't matter. That, as someone who was raised interfaith, I'll never be seen as an equal.

I look at my feet, take a deep breath, and look back up.

I'm ready to say something to Eli, perhaps to tell him the history of interfaith relationships or maybe just utter a stream of creative curses, when Saron speaks.

"I was told, in temple, that I'm not a real Jew 'cause of the color of my skin. Like you've got to be some pasty white dude to read the Torah. Like there isn't a whole community of Ethiopian Jews. Like there aren't Jews of color."

"It's a problem here too," Shira adds. "In Israel there is much racism."

Saron touches her Star of David necklace. "I'm proud I'm Black, and I'm proud I'm Jewish.

"After everything we've seen today," she continues, "how can we keep fighting? Why are we awful to each other?"

We're quiet again. The air feels heavy in the room, and my bones feel heavy in my body.

Chaya breaks the silence. "If anyone else wants to talk, we are here. Your Madricha, your Madrich. We are here.

"Dinner is at seven. Now you can go. Rest."

PUT ON A HAPPY FACE

I'm on my bed with the covers pulled over my head when I feel someone sit down beside me.

"What is wrong with you? Are you sick?" Saron asks.

I pull the covers down just enough so that I can see her. "No."

"You look a little sick," she says.

I sit up. "I'm not. I'm just trying to nap."

She shrugs. "I was thinking we could talk plans for tonight," she says. "Since Sammy is in the shower."

Plans. Matchmaking plans. Because I thought I could fix Max.

I can't even fix myself.

"I don't think we really need to," I start. "Let them just figure it out themselves."

Saron laughs. "You're funny," she says. Then she continues. "I did some digging, meaning I talked briefly to Jess, and I found out that we're going to have free time again tonight. Which will be perfect. I'm going to do makeovers, and we're all going to go out dancing. There's nothing more romantic than dancing with someone."

"I don't think that's technically true," I say.

"Pretty sure it is." She gets up off the bed and walks over to her suitcase. "I've already started thinking about all our outfits. You're going to wear that black off-the-shoulder dress I know you've been hoarding, no excuses. I'm thinking I might try to get Sammy to wear something I brought." She holds up a short dress covered in gold sequins. "Is this too much? I packed it for New Year's. Anyway, I'll do makeup too. We're going to have to eat pretty fast if we want to get it all done, but I don't think that'll be a problem."

I don't know how to stop this. I should just tell her I'm not going tonight. I should have told her I was sick; the excuse was right there.

I could tell her that Max doesn't need to be happy because he's actually awful and deserves to be sad forever, but that might not go over well.

I do the easier thing: I don't say anything.

Not while Saron plans, not while we have dinner at a table across the room from Max. Not even when Saron announces that we're going to go back to the room for makeovers.

"Oh, we don't need to get all dressed up," Sammy says. "We went out last night. Really, we could just stay in."

"Tally was with her family, remember? We can't deprive her of a fun, non-family outing," Saron says.

I don't think this is anywhere near the realm of what I need, but I follow them upstairs because there's nothing I can say that will make sense. Nothing I can do to stop it.

How could I even try to explain? If I tell them what's wrong, they'll start to look at me like . . . well, like I was looking at Max when I thought he hadn't applied to any schools.

Maybe I should tell them the truth. Maybe I should let them try to fix me.

Maybe I'll just excuse myself and find a dumpster to sit in. I have options.

By the time we're getting off the elevator, I know there's only one thing I can realistically do without ruining this trip. I'll have to play along and pretend that everything is normal.

Nothing has changed. I can keep pretending that nothing has changed.

"I'm thinking winged eyeliner, Tally Mark, and a neutral lip, maybe a brown mauve? And of course, we're going to need to deal with your hair," Saron says as we walk into the room.

She's talking directly to me now. I should answer, since everything is normal.

"This?" I ask, swishing my ponytail. "We have to deal with this?"

Saron rolls her eyes. "Yes, that."

"It takes about an hour to straighten," I warn.

"You think I always kept my hair like this? Quit complaining."

She decides to do my makeup first, so I can straighten my hair while she works on Sammy. I'm apparently not allowed to look in the mirror until the whole thing is put together or I will ruin the surprise.

"What you have to understand," Saron says, applying my eyeliner, "is that makeovers aren't about changing who you are as a person. Those movies where a girl loses her glasses and ponytail and is therefore suddenly popular and desirable? Absolutely ridiculous. Are you trying to tell me a girl isn't worth anything if she has a ponytail and glasses?" She frowns. "What it is about is confidence. Makeup can be like an armor, if you use it right. A makeover? That's about looking a little different, giving up control of your appearance, and seeing how you feel. Like a really low-key Halloween where someone else picks out your costume. Look up," she directs. "I'm going to do your mascara now."

Sammy walks out from the bathroom with her hair in a simple braid down her back just as Saron is finishing my lips. "Oh, you really went all out," she says.

"What did you do?" I ask, worried.

Saron shakes her head. "Confidence, Tally Mark. Confidence."

They send me to the corner, next to the plug with Sammy's travel converter in it. I sit on the floor and watch as Saron works carefully on Sammy. I think she might be right.

I think about the other part of what she said too—the thing about the movies. I love those sorts of scenes, but I guess they can be pretty cringey. I agree with part of Saron's rant. Confidence is important, but I think, on a certain level, the confidence is always there. The makeover just gives them an excuse to show off what was hidden the whole time.

I'm still finishing my hair when Sammy and Saron move on to outfits. Saron holds up her New Year's dress for Sammy, a short dress with gold sequins, thin straps, and a low neckline.

"Oh, I'll just wear something I brought with me," Sammy says.

"It's totally fine; I know it looks fancy, but I just got it at a thrift store," Saron says.

Sammy shakes her head. "It's not that. I actually choose to dress more conservatively. It's something that connects me to my faith."

Has she been dressing conservatively this whole time? I honestly didn't notice. When I picture Jewish people dressing for their faith, it's usually more conservative: wigs, leggings, hats. Maybe yarmulkes for boys, at least. Sammy's style is flowy and cute and very much her own.

Saron moves on, looking for her own outfit. She picks a floral wrap dress for herself.

"Is that mine?" I ask.

The cap sleeves are too big on her shoulders, drooping down to her upper arm, and she's wrapped the belt around her waist twice.

Saron smiles. "I wanted a costume too."

I get a chance to look in the mirror only as we're about to walk out to meet the boys in the lobby. With my hair down and straightened, it falls to my chest. I didn't realize it had gotten that long; the curls usually disguise the length with their general mess. With the makeup, I look like someone else, a person with much more defined cheekbones and cat eyes. A character. I can play a character.

I run my hands against the full skirt of my dress. This is my costume. I'm wearing armor.

I can do this.

OUT TONIGHT

I can't do this. The first person I see when we get to the lobby is Max. I can't be near him right now; he'll give it all away. He'll tell them that I'm sad and broken.

He doesn't say anything as we join the group. Instead, it's Saron who speaks.

"What the hell are you wearing?" she asks, eyeing Joshua.

"Funny, right?" he says, patting his stomach. He's wearing a fake tuxedo shirt that looks like it has been passed down through at least three generations based on the amount of wear.

From Saron's face, I can tell she does not in fact think it's funny. "I told you guys we were dressing up," she says. "I can picture it. We were in line for food. You responded to me. Did you think I was joking?"

"I am dressed up!" Joshua tugs at his novelty shirt, which is too tight and riding up his back. "You just don't get it."

"I told him not to wear it, but . . ." Gabriel waves toward

his friend. "Never listens." He's in a white polo and jeans, casual enough that I worry Saron will scold him, too, but she doesn't say anything. At least it's better than a tuxedo shirt.

"Are we all ready?" Sammy cuts in.

Joshua shakes his head. "Just waiting on—David! Over here!" he calls out. "Yeah, we can head out."

I look at David as he walks over to join our group. He's wearing a button down and dark jeans. Did she know he was coming and didn't tell me? Did Saron corner him and tell him he had to look nice too? I'm trying not to think about the way David looks in his shirt or the fact that there's a bit of stubble on his face, which makes him look different. Not a bad different. Just different.

"Hey," he says. He waves like he's introducing himself. "I hope it's okay if I tag along. I promise I'm not a narc. You can go as wild as you want."

"Sounds like a narc to me," Saron says, but then she goes over and pats him on the back. "Come on, this will be fun." With that, she starts walking toward the exit of the hotel.

Joshua and Gabriel follow.

"You two realize that you're too young to go to a club?" David asks.

"He is a narc!" Joshua gasps.

Saron shakes her head. "You're the one who literally invited one of the staff members when you were doing something against the rules. Have fun with your consequences."

We leave the sixteen-year-olds behind and head to the club.

I haven't talked to David since the beach, not really. It's not like I was avoiding him. We were just at the cemetery and Yad Vashem and it would have been super inappropriate to bring up my issues at either of those stops. Plus, what was I going to say? "Sorry I lost us the game"? "I was just panicking"? No thank you.

He ends up falling into step with me.

"Hey," he says. "Having fun?"

"Walking to a club?"

He's quiet for a second before lowering his voice. "I just . . . wanted to check in. Are you okay?" He's got a full-on serious look on his face like he can tell I'm in the middle of a breakdown.

"Why wouldn't I be?" I ask, light and breezy. Totally normal.

"I just thought . . . You know what, never mind."

He lets it drop.

The club is only a short walk away, so I don't really have to deal with any more small talk.

"Rivkah suggested this place," Saron says as we enter.

There's a dance floor and a bar and too-loud music. The bar seems sort of packed, so most of our group immediately makes their way to the dance floor. Saron executes what I have to assume is a fully choreographed dance routine as Max films the whole thing on his phone and Sammy laughs at his side. Somehow it's just David and me standing there, near the bar.

"Do you want anything? Water?" he asks.

"Yeah, sure." He just asked if I wanted water; that's nothing, but it was also sort of thoughtful. A lot of people forget that I don't drink and I mentioned it only once, when we were at the winery, so that probably means he was paying attention. Which means he likes me, which means I'm overthinking things again. *Water is water—calm down.*

It takes a while for the bartender to pay us any attention. David orders a beer and my water, and then we're standing off to the side. Not talking. Not that we could talk anyway; it's so freaking loud.

"Dance?" he asks over the music.

I nod because what else are we supposed to do here?

We find the group pretty easily once we get to the dance floor. Sammy is now wearing the #IVEGOTCHUTZPAH banner around her shoulders, which Saron is holding from either end, like it's a crucial dance accessory.

We all dance in a group to music that is mostly in Hebrew. David is right next to me. I'm swaying my hips and putting my hands in the air because I don't want to look like I'm bad at dancing, but then I'm worried that it's all too suggestive and, honestly, I'm still not that great of a dancer.

We're like this for a long time or no time at all, I can't tell in here. I don't think time even exists in clubs. There's nothing but the sweat and the pounding music and the fear that some drunk person is going to dance up on me at any moment. I need a break. I think about asking Saron if she wants to go to the bathroom because safety in numbers notoriously prevents being kidnapped in foreign clubs, but she looks like she's having fun. So I turn away by myself. I'll be fine; I do know some minimal self-defense.

David follows me off the dance floor.

"Want company?" he yell-asks over the music.

"Sure," I yell-respond. I guess the bathroom idea is off the table.

"We could get some air," he yell-suggests.

I nod.

We walk out of the club, and it's a little chilly outside. I rub my arms, questioning the short sleeves and fully exposed shoulders.

"Having fun?" he asks. This time his voice is at a normal noise level.

"Yeah," I say.

"You're not really selling it. You might want to try something like, 'Wow, I could go all night! *Woo!*'"

He's such a dork.

"I don't think clubs are my thing."

He laughs. "Same. Give me a low-key party over a trendy nightclub any day."

"See, I'm more of a *hang out at home with some Jenga* kind of girl."

"Your wild nature never ceases to amaze me." He pauses, absentmindedly fidgeting with a button on his shirt. "You're having fun, though, right? Because you don't have to stay. Shoot, that sounds like I'm telling you to leave." He makes this exaggerated *my bad* sort of expression. "We could walk back. That's what I meant."

"No, no. I'm good. Just needed a break."

"Okay," he says. "I've got a game for our break. Would You Rather."

"Basic rules, I suppose?"

"Yes, keeping it simple."

"You go first."

"Would you rather spend all night in a club or get attacked by a bear?"

"Bear, hands down. I think I could take it," I say. "All right, club or have me splash you with that salty ocean water for an hour straight."

"Ocean water. You'd have so much fun, the pain would be worth it. Plus, I think I've mastered protecting my eyes." He mimes dodging out of the way of my nonexistent splashes. "Hmm . . . let's see. Club or give up hummus forever?"

"I guess I could survive a little club time. Five minutes, tops."

He smiles. "That means I won."

"You certainly did not," I say, rightfully offended. "I take it back; I'm giving up hummus."

"Can't do that—it's against the rules."

"Well, I didn't know the secret objective was to get me to choose the club."

"It was implied." He nods to himself.

I smack his arm in that *you're too much* sort of way. Which is kind of flirty, isn't it?

"So clubs are really the worst-case scenario?" he asks.

"Obviously," I say. "There's the grinding and the gross

people and the chance that at any moment, some sloppy drunk is going to spill their drink on you. And the noise. Oh, the noise."

"You sound like an expert."

"I was paying close attention while we were in there." I add, "I like the company, though." I mean everyone, the whole group, but he must think I'm talking about just him because there's this look in his eyes. They're wider, hopeful even.

"I like the company too." He means me; I know he means me. It's the way he's looking at me, though I can't tell if it's kind or expectant.

There's a pause. One of those heavy pauses where you can feel your heart beating too fast and your thoughts racing too quickly. I think this is when we are supposed to kiss. In a musical, this is definitely when the romantic leads would kiss. So I get on my tiptoes and give him a quick peck on the cheek.

He smiles. He takes my face in his hands and bends down to kiss my lips.

I try kissing him back, but I don't feel anything, not like every book and movie and friend has ever explained you're supposed to feel. Instead, it's like I'm entirely outside of the situation. Maybe that's not completely true because I can feel the actual physical aspects, his lips, a little chapped, against mine, his hands on my face. I can smell the slight aroma of beer still clinging to his breath, taste it a little too. I can hear the smacking. The lip-smacking sound is the worst. *Smack smack smack.* I can't stand it, *smack*; it's so loud, *smack*; and my body starts shaking, *smack*, and I can't breathe, *smack*.

I can't breathe this needs to stop I can't breathe.

He pulls away. "Tally, are you all right?"

I don't think I am because my breaths are so sharp and fast and my body is really shaking now. "I need. I need to go. I—*don't touch me!*—I need to go."

I want to run, get away, lock myself in the hotel bathroom, but I don't know the way back. I'm in the club again; when did I get back into the club? It's too loud and I can't think and I can't breathe. I need Cat.

I have Max. He's not on the dance floor and he's not in the girls' bathroom and why would he be in the girls' bathroom, you idiot? I'm never going to find him and I am stuck and I am broken.

I see him standing at the bar.

"Tally, what's going on?"

I should probably respond, but I don't even know what's going on or why my body is acting this way, so instead I put my head on his chest. My face feels wet now. Am I crying? Am I crying all over my brother's shirt? He takes me in his arms and holds me tight and whispers, "You're okay. I've got you; you're okay. Let's go back. I've got you; you're okay."

I don't even remember walking to the hotel. I don't remember getting on the elevator. I don't remember getting to my room. I'm alone in the bathroom now, the door closed. Max is just outside, waiting in the room.

I look in the mirror. My lipstick looks smeared. I need to get it all off. Now. I'm using a makeup remover wipe, but it's not working fast enough and my lips aren't clean enough and I feel dirty, gross, and it has nothing to do with David and everything to do with me.

This is a panic attack, I realize. I'm having a panic attack. It will pass.

It will never end.

I look in the mirror again and I'm a mess and I'm terrible and I ruin everything. I can't even talk to Cat about it. I can never talk to Cat about it. I can never talk to Cat again.

WAVING THROUGH A WINDOW

I'm alone because I told Max I needed to sleep, and he believed me. So now I'm lying on the bed with the covers pulled over my head. Cat and I used to do that during sleepovers. We'd pull the covers over our heads and talk. We called it the bubble.

The bubble is safe.

I'm coming down; I'm coming back. *Check in.* I can breathe again, and my heart rate has slowed. I'm not shaking. I'm physically fine.

I'll never be fine again.

What is wrong with me? I can't even kiss a boy without spiraling into a panic attack. What would Cat tell me to do? Probably to have some chocolate or try to write so I can work out my feelings.

I take out the popping chocolate I've been saving in my bag and go back under the covers. I eat the whole bar, slowly, letting each piece dissolve on my tongue until it's nothing but fizzing sugar.

The chocolate doesn't help, which feels like a betrayal.

The truth is, I don't want to work out my feelings. First of all, I have too many of them. How am I supposed to deal with what happened with David tonight *and* Max secretly applying to schools *and* being far from home *and* going to Yad Vashem *and and and*—

I have to prioritize tonight. I managed to take this momentous life event, my first kiss, and turn it into something catastrophic. What happens if someone asks about my first kiss? I have the absolute worst story. How am I supposed to face David now? How am I supposed to go through life without being able to kiss anyone?

How am I supposed to deal with all of this without my best friend?

I picture Cat next to me in the bubble, ready to talk about the kiss, and it hits me again, the sudden stabbing realization that she's not here. I immediately shove the thought away, but then another takes its place.

It's like you can't mourn.

I can't, I can't, I can't.

I'm broken. That's it. It's as simple as that. I'm just a broken person. A lost cause. Broken.

That's when it happens. It's like the little voice that I've been missing inside my head wakes up.

I throw the covers off from over my head and reach to the floor to get my purse. I take out the notebook Cat gave me.

And I write.

IT'S QUIET UPTOWN

I skip breakfast the next morning. I'm not ready to leave my bed, but I have to pack and I have to bring my suitcase down and I have to get on the bus.

Saron and Sammy packed already. I pretended to be asleep as they wheeled their suitcases out the door and down to breakfast. They whispered to each other about whether they should wake me up or not, but Saron said I needed sleep. I'd meet them down there. I'd be fine.

We're going to the Dead Sea, and all I can picture is a bunch of corpses floating in the water. Everything feels dead now anyway. Somewhere in my brain, I know this is supposed to be a fun day. It's New Year's Eve. We're going swimming and then driving to the desert to camp.

But I can't pretend I'm fine anymore.

I'm going to have to see David. I'm going to have to face the dumpster fire of a mess that I've created. What exactly am I supposed to say? "Hey, David. Sorry for the freak-out.

Weird, right? Who kisses someone and then has a panic attack? *HAHAHA*, let's never speak again. 'Kay, bye."

Cat would know what to say. She always knew what to say.

As I pack up my things, I keep imagining what it will be like to see David. I fold my clothes and he's standing there, too tall, in the hotel lobby. I gather my toiletries, which are scattered across the bathroom counter, and there are those dark curls, visible from the front of the bus. Then I think about his face, the way his eyes were wide before we kissed and now, in my mind, they seem flecked with gold, bright, brighter than they were on the dark Israeli street. The concern, *Tally, are you all right?* and he looked so genuine and gentle and he tried to touch my arm, carefully, like maybe I needed comfort, some assurance that everything was in fact all right, but then I screamed at him and I left.

Is that what I did? Is that what he did? I don't even know. I don't even know what really happened. Why don't I know what really happened? Why am I like this?

Now I imagine him angry. He's whispering to Jess, telling her about how I'm a monster. His eyes are sharp as he stares at me. Or maybe he'll just ignore me completely? Maybe this is no big deal because it was just a kiss, barely a kiss, and maybe he didn't even want it in the first place. Maybe he was drunk and he won't even remember what happened. Maybe he was just trying to be nice to this weird girl on this trip where he's working and it would be easier to just kiss me on the lips than let that awkward cheek peck be the end of it.

It's 7:57, and I'm supposed to be on the bus in three minutes. Probably time to head downstairs.

"Look, a straggler," Jess says. She's standing there alone. "Hope you're feeling better—Max told us about your migraine. Batya will help you get the suitcase into the bottom of the bus; make sure you have everything you need for the Dead Sea with you. Bathing suit, change of clothes, sunscreen, hat, water bottle. Everyone's right outside the door and to the left."

My migraine? Max created an excuse.

That makes it even worse, because I wasn't there this morning and they were talking about me. He shouldn't be taking care of me in the first place. That's not how this works; that's not what this trip was supposed to be about.

It was supposed to be about . . . applying to schools. Which he did. Without telling me. Because apparently he's fine and I'm not.

I walk onto the bus.

David is a few rows away. He isn't looking my way; he's in the middle of talking to Chaya about something. I need to sit before he looks over. I need to hide. I need—

"I saved you a seat," Max says. He's sitting right in the front, his carry-on bag in the spot next to him. He moves it to the floor to make room for me.

I sit down.

"Are you feeling better?" he asks, his voice quiet.

I shrug.

"That's not really a response."

No, it isn't. Because I don't have a response ready that he would want to hear. Plus, we're on a bus, surrounded by other people, and David is three rows away.

"Can we talk later? I'm really tired," I say. Which isn't technically a lie. I stayed up drafting a new song, scratching out words and moving around lines. When I finally stopped, I couldn't turn off my brain. I was still awake when Sammy and Saron got back from the club, still awake even after they had fallen asleep.

Max nods.

Before he can say anything else, I pull out my headphones.

It takes us two hours to get to the Dead Sea Spa. I keep my eyes closed for most of the ride, listening to the music. I don't want to see anything right now.

The "spa" is basically a low-grade recreational center with a store that features all the Dead Sea–related products you could ever need. Everything is white and sterile-looking under the harsh lights. There's a changing area that has showers we will very much need after we coat ourselves in the mineral-rich mud, which is supposedly great for your skin. Outside the changing area, there are signs, written in English and Hebrew, for a cafeteria in the basement.

I put on my bathing suit, the same yellow one-piece I wore rafting and to the beach. I hate this bathing suit; I hate these cutouts; I hate the way it makes me look. I hate the fact that Cat picked it out.

"It's sunny," she said in the store.

"In that I will look like I'm the size of the actual sun if I wear it?"

She took both my cheeks and squeezed them like she was a grandma talking to a baby. "In that you will look radiant."

I cross my arms over my stomach, my hands covering the skin exposed through the cutouts. I certainly don't feel radiant right now.

Chaya and Jess are sitting outside the dressing rooms, around a white plastic table, guarding the bags.

"You two aren't going?" I ask. I grip my towel, wrapped over my shoulders like a cape.

"Batya and David will be by the water. We stay. We've done this before," Chaya says, as though this isn't a big deal.

They might have the right idea. I shiver when we walk outside. It's colder today, but I have to buck up. When else am I going to have a chance to visit the Dead Sea?

There are passenger trams that are waiting to take us down to the beach, and they look like stretched-out golf carts. I can see David up ahead as he gets on the first bus. I get on the second.

"There you are," Saron says, taking the spot next to me. "How are you feeling? Max told us about your migraine."

What did he do? Hold a press conference to lie to everyone so he could cover up my panic attack?

"I'm okay," I say.

She adjusts her towel, rolling it tighter around her waist. "The mud will help," she adds. "It has all kinds of healing properties. You'll feel amazing when we're done here."

If only she knew how much healing I need.

The first thing I notice as we get closer is the smell: the putrid stench of sulfur. Not exactly the piña colada aroma I associate with the beach. When we stop, even the coastline looks weird. The sand is crystallized and white around the water. We have to keep on our sandals so our feet don't get hurt.

We get in the water first. The thing about the Dead Sea is that the salt content is so high that it basically lifts you up and makes you feel weightless. It also makes the water painful. We were told not to shave before coming here, but some people clearly did not listen, Joshua among them. He leaves the water almost immediately. "Why? Why did no one tell me? That is stinging devil water," he says, gently rubbing his upper lip.

"I told you it wasn't worth it. You don't even have a mustache," Gabriel says.

"Stop being jealous of my abundant facial hair."

Once we're out of the water, Saron gathers us around a particularly muddy area. "All right, I need a photo. That means you need to be entirely covered in mud." We look at her, waiting for her to continue. She lets out a big sigh. "So cover yourselves in mud."

I can see David walking over. I don't want David to come over. He's looking at me, a little expectantly. There's pressure in his look. I hate the pressure in his look.

He is already smeared with mud, and I hate that, too, for some reason. I hate that I hate it. I hate that my brain isn't making any sense right now. *All* of us are covering ourselves with mud; I know all of us are doing this. So why is it different with him?

"Anyone need any help?" he asks.

Does he mean me? Does he want to touch me again? I can't do that; I can't let that happen.

"Yes, but not from you. You're already covered," Saron says. "Go get us a clean person to take a picture."

David obliges.

By the time we have a very clean and completely dry Rivkah taking our picture, everyone looks vaguely like a swamp-monster version of themselves. Rivkah has the right idea; she's wearing jeans and a jacket right now. I am envious of her warmth.

I wait to see where David is going to stand so I can position myself on the other side.

"I brought something special for this moment," Joshua announces. He unfolds his towel to reveal the banner.

"Yes!" Gabriel says. "This is going to look great."

Joshua and Gabriel hold the banner, kneeling on the sharp, crystalized buildup at the edge of the water. They're trying to be careful with it, but they have already left smears of mud around the edges.

"Say 'best day ever,'" Saron directs.

"Best day ever!" the group chimes.

I glance at David, then back to the camera. I can feel the breath catch in my throat. Quietly, a little after everyone else, I say, "Best day ever."

Rivkah takes the picture.

———

When we get back on the bus, I sit with Saron. I don't want to deal with Max right now.

She has her sketch pad out and is quietly drawing, which works for me. I can go back to listening to my music. But a half hour into the drive, I feel a tap on my arm.

"I need a sounding board," Saron says. She hands me her sketch pad.

There are three different silhouettes drawn on the page. One dress is off the shoulder with wide, flowing sleeves; another is short and boxy. The last one has a wide slit in the skirt up to the thigh and a low-cut neckline. The design is drawn on the side, a set of cartoon zombies on pool floats.

"I've been trying to find the perfect idea, the right inspiration, but I don't think I'm there yet. This is just too . . . literal. I can't even settle on the style I want for the dress." She sighs. "What do you think?"

"I think you're trivializing something very serious," I say.

"What?" she asks.

"The dead bodies for the Dead Sea. That isn't fashion. That isn't clever."

She looks at me, confused. "You mean the cartoon zombies?" She says it like I'm being ridiculous. Like this is some big joke.

"It's not funny," I continue. "Death isn't funny. Death isn't beautiful. Have you seen a dead body before?"

"Have you?" she asks. I can't tell if she is angry with me or concerned.

I ignore her question. "Why do you always draw your

models like this?" I ask. "They're practically sticks. That's not how real people look."

"Okay," she says, the word slow and drawn out.

"I just don't think this idea is working."

"Clearly," she says. She closes her sketch pad.

We don't talk for the rest of the ride.

WHAT'S WRONG WITH ME?

Our group is properly in the desert now. I've never been in a desert before. The soil, a dirt so light I wonder if it's actually sand, stretches up to our tents and out beyond my eyesight. It seems endless, like we're lost, completely disconnected from the outside world.

Or rather, it seemed that way until we walked into the resort that we're staying in. The place has sectioned-off tents, so large they can fit an entire tour group, surrounding the main section of the stay. Our group dropped off our day bags in our tent already. Tent, singular. Meaning, I'm supposed to sleep in the same space as the boy I made a fool of myself in front of. Right.

Our tent has a thin layer of mismatched rugs to separate us from the desert ground. We each got a small mat and a sleeping bag.

The middle of the resort sports an even larger tent that

functions as a mini restaurant, a small store, a seating area with wooden tables and benches and bonfires, and camp-style bathrooms.

This is our Bedouin Tent Night. There are at least three other groups here right now. Bedouins are a group of nomadic Arabic people who live in the desert to this day. I have to believe this isn't an authentic version of their experience.

We're in the large, tented area that is set aside for eating, sitting at the small wooden tables organized throughout, which are so low that you have to sit on the floor to reach the food.

Saron did not sit at my table. That feels like a childish thing to be worried about, but I sat down first, which means she chose to go somewhere else. I can see her across the tent, already eating. She says something to Jess, and Jess laughs. She's probably making fun of me now. Not that I don't deserve the ridicule.

"What are we doing tonight?" Joshua asks, grabbing bits of spiced rice from the communal platter in the middle of the table, using bread like a serving spoon. We were told that we were supposed to eat with our hands, but I suspect that the custom doesn't excuse the mess around Joshua's plate.

"Tonight?" Gabriel asks from his side, the table in front of him spotless. "Don't we have to be up at five AM?"

We do. Tomorrow we're going on a hike up Masada to see the sunrise.

"It's New Year's Eve!" Joshua says. "We have to do something."

Here's the problem with New Year's Eve: there's often drinking and always kissing. It's basically the law of the holiday. So inevitably, someone will be kissing someone else, and then there will be that awful lip-smacking noise again. Or worse, we will all gather for the big countdown to the New Year and David will be standing nearby, and then I'll have to think about kissing him and maybe he'll expect to kiss me again and then—

Thought spiral.

It'll just be easier if we all go to sleep before midnight.

Which is why I say, "I'm out. I want to rest before tomorrow."

Max, who is sitting next to me, looks over. "You're going to go to sleep before midnight on New Year's?" he asks.

"What part of *five AM hike* do you not understand?"

This does not seem to stop Joshua. "What if we stage a fake countdown?" he proposes. "We can have a dance party leading up to it and . . . Wait! Do you guys think anyone here has any fireworks?"

"Dude, no," Gabriel says.

"We could at least do a game night," Max offers. "Just something low-key and fun to celebrate. I *did* move Cards Against Humanity from my suitcase to my carry-on."

He's speaking to the whole group, but his eyes are on me. I guess a couple of rounds of Cards Against Humanity couldn't hurt, and it might be funny to see the Israelis play.

After dinner, everyone settles in for the night. I set up my mat at the edge of the tent. Max is by my side. I watch as

Saron takes her overnight bag and places it a few rows away. Of course she doesn't want to sleep near me. She's probably sick of me as both a roommate and a person.

It's easier this way, though. It's easier to end things early.

I go to the communal bathroom alone to use one of the few changing rooms. I put on my Captain Marvel pajamas, which I love because they make me feel like I can smash the patriarchy. Except, the moment after I change, I start to worry that this isn't the right choice. Should I be wearing some sort of fancy dress, with glitter or sequins? Will everyone start laughing when I walk into the tent because I missed the memo on the whole New Year's Eve thing and somehow Joshua has arranged an all-out party with fireworks?

My breath catches. No. No, I cannot have a panic attack over this.

By the time I get back, Max has already started organizing the game, and I'm not the only one in pajamas.

There's a big circle of players forming inside the tent. This is the biggest game I have ever seen. I mean, there are teams, plural, and still way too many players. The Israelis are dispersed among the groups.

I can hear Saron a few groups over. She's on a team with Rivkah and Sammy.

"So you want to pick the funniest answer, but you need to know the other person's humor. Which is basically pointless, since most of us are virtual strangers. So really, everyone is going to try to out-offend one another," Saron explains. Rivkah nods as she looks through the cards.

"'Pixelated Bu-cake'?"

"Oy. Okay, that means . . ."

David is at the other side of the tent; he's on a team with Jess and Shira. I don't know if I can play a game with him. Can I play a game with him? I can't even look at him without freaking out, and now we're supposed to have fun together?

I sit down to play. I'm on a team with Max and Batya. We play well. It's a giant group, but we still win two of the first five rounds.

But then David's team is up.

I look at him. I don't want to look at him, but he's the one holding the card. He's the one I'm supposed to listen to. I tell myself that there's a whole group and we've been together before, but for some reason, the simple act of looking at him makes me want to cry, which is irrational and I recognize that it is irrational.

I realize he's already reading the prompt.

"'. . . try surprising him with blank instead,'" David reads.

Try surprising him with a panic attack instead. Try surprising him by running away. Try surprising him by avoiding all contact with him for as long as humanly possible even though you are on a group trip through Israel and he is one of the staff members.

I need to get out.

"I'm going to the bathroom," I whisper to Max.

"Want me to come?" he asks.

"To the girls' bathroom? No. I'm fine—keep playing."

I walk to the seating area, where there are a bunch of circular wooden picnic tables. There are a few other people around, but I manage to find an empty spot so I can sit by myself.

I have my phone, but there's no Wi-Fi, and I left my headphones in my bag, so after I sit down, I go through some old pictures that I have saved.

My lock screen is of Cat and me. It's from the last school musical we were in together. *Annie*. She was Miss Hannigan, and I was an orphan. I always liked it better in the background, but that would never do for her. In the picture, we both have our makeup and costumes on. She's holding flowers.

There are more pictures from that night, a couple from the performance that my dad took and others from after the musical, in our pajamas with the makeup still on, baking cookies.

I keep looking at pictures of her on my phone. There are some awkward photos from middle school where we both have greasy hair and then ones of other shows and other sleepovers.

I'm not really paying attention to anything else when I hear someone say, "Tally?"

David. David is standing in front of me. He has his hands in his pockets, and he looks even taller now that I'm sitting.

"Hi," he says.

"Hey." Is my voice shaky? I feel like my voice is shaky.

"I noticed you weren't playing. Thought someone might have kidnapped you."

"A stranger in a van did try to bribe me with promises of Scrabble. I'm lucky to be alive."

"Glad you're safe now," he says. "Mind if I sit?"

I could say that I mind. I could say that I want him to go away forever.

I pat the seat next to me.

He sits down and takes a deep breath. "I just wanted to apologize. About last night—"

"David, you really don't have to—"

"No, look, I clearly misread the situation, and I should have asked you first, and I never wanted to make you feel uncomfortable, and—"

"David, stop. You didn't do anything wrong." I pull my legs up to my chest and wrap my arms around my knees. "It was me."

Because it *was* me. I initiated it and then panicked. I should feel bad about that. Here is this nice and caring boy, and I can't even get my act together enough to kiss him when he actually wanted to kiss me.

I think my heart is racing a little.

"No, it wasn't. I should have made sure it was what you wanted."

"I thought it was," I say softly.

My heart is definitely racing, and no, I don't need to freak out again. I take a deep breath. "Look, this is embarrassing. I know I'm way too old for this, but that was my first kiss."

He looks at me with his kind, muddy eyes. "My first kiss wasn't until I was a senior. I was eighteen. There's really nothing weird about that."

I look back at my knees. "I guess." I pause. "It's just. It feels weird. You know, I haven't even held hands with anyone."

"And we jumped right into kissing? Should've taken it back a step," he jokes. "Sorry, was that jerky? I was trying to make you laugh, but now I think I'm just being a jerk."

"Total jerk," I say.

He looks at me, and it's a Serious Look, like he's trying to figure me out and gauge my emotional status and maybe rip a hole in the space–time continuum. "It really isn't weird. Some people have those epic love stories in high school or in college, and some people don't. Some people take their time. Some people meet the love of their lives in a preschool classroom, and some people meet them in a retirement community. Some people don't want romantic relationships at all. You're not weird; you are living your own story."

He sounds so genuine, like he's finishing off some inspirational TED Talk. I start laughing.

"Wow. That was . . ."

"Heartfelt? Motivational?" he offers.

"Cheesy," I say. "Mac and cheesy. Mozzarella cheesy sticks. A whole pie of cheesy pizza."

He smiles. "I'm going to claim a win. Got you to laugh."

"Sure, Mr. Grilled Cheesy."

"You going to keep this up?"

"Of course. Cheesycake. Wait, have you heard of fondue? It's a pot of melted cheesy." I'm still laughing and fine, I do feel marginally better.

"Yeah, yeah, make fun of me." He's still smiling. "Okay, well, I can go if you want me to; I just wanted to check in."

He starts to stand up.

"You can stay," I say. "I like talking to you."

"I like talking to you too," he says.

"How about this? What if we're friends," I suggest. "Takes any weird pressure off."

"Sounds like a plan." He actually puts out his hand, like we're making some official pact. I shake it. We've touched again, but that's okay, because we're friends now. Everything is super platonic.

"All right, friend. What do you want to talk about?" he asks. "Something cheese related?"

"I think we can do better," I say.

We talk until the New Year.

SUNRISE, SUNSET

Admittedly, stopping someone in the middle of a hike up a mountain before the sun is even up might not have been the best choice, but I need to apologize. If I can talk to David, I can definitely talk to Saron.

"Hey," I start, walking in line with her.

She takes a swig from her water bottle. "Yes?"

"I, well. I wanted to say that I'm sorry I was the worst yesterday. It wasn't about your designs."

"I had, in fact, made that leap," she says.

"So," I continue, "I'm sorry. For being awful yesterday."

Saron stops walking. "Want to talk about why you were being awful?"

How should I even respond to that? Should I tell her everything that happened? About my fight with Max? My panic attack? Should I tell her about Cat?

"Not particularly," I say.

For a second, I think she might yell at me and tell me to get lost forever or demand a full explanation, but then she laughs.

"Been there, Tally Mark," she says, putting her arm around my shoulder. "Now, let's get to the top before we miss out on the sunrise. I've heard the hike is worth it."

We start walking again.

"I'm happy you found me," she adds. "I have news."

"Oh?"

"While you were off doing whatever the hell you were doing last night, something happened."

"Yes?"

"Something big," she continues.

"Oh, just tell me; this is too much."

She smiles. "I decided to go rogue. I staged a whole pretend countdown so we could go to sleep at a reasonable time. I made this big deal out of how everyone needed to find someone to kiss at pretend midnight."

"And?"

She winks. "Mission accomplished. Max and Sammy are officially set. The match has been made."

Mission accomplished. I don't know how to feel. I guess he can be happy now.

I think about all the schools Max applied to . . . the ones out of state, even out of the country. I guess maybe he was happy all along. He doesn't need me.

It's starting to get lighter, and I wonder if we really are going to miss the sunrise. The path evens out, and I see other tour groups already settling in.

Gabriel is taking out the banner for a sunrise picture

while Joshua gets his speakers ready so he can play "Circle of Life" as soon as we see the sun. I know this because he turns to Gabriel and says, "What if you hold the banner up like it's Simba when the song plays?" and the two fist-bump. In the meantime, they have "Here Comes the Sun" playing on repeat. Max, Sammy, Saron, David, and I find a spot to sit. Jess and Chaya are up on some rocks behind us.

We watch as orange and pink break through the dark horizon, the fuzzy glow of the sun getting bigger and higher. The sunrise is clear, and I remind myself not to look too long because it will hurt my eyes.

We all take pictures. I don't think there's a way to really capture what it's like, sitting at the top of Masada as the sun rises over the desert. On my phone, the sun looks small, a pinprick compared to the sight in front of us, and the focus switches, first too dark, so that the mix of colors in the sky is the only thing that is clear on my screen, and then too light, the colors now washed out.

Then we pose with one another. Max asks Sammy to take a picture of the two of us, and we stand with our backs to the sun, smiling.

There are only so many versions of the same picture you can take, so Chaya gathers us back together. "Now, I have a thing to show you," she says. We walk around a few ruins and a bathroom that is clearly new, installed for tourists. We stop in front of a giant cavern.

A very steep giant cavern. A very steep giant cavern with thin steps. I'm pretty sure I'm about to trip and fall and break every single bone in my body.

"We go down," Chaya says excitedly, because she apparently finds humor in my pain.

Luckily, I don't actually plummet down the stairs and break my body, but that is largely thanks to the handrail, which I clutch the whole way down.

Chaya has us sit right on the ground, which is leaving a nice chalk outline all over my leggings. She tells us the history of Masada, how this was a fortress, and when the Romans came to attack, there was a mass suicide. How almost a thousand people decided to die rather than be captured.

This is technically not historically accurate.

There's no archeological proof that this is exactly what happened in Masada. I knew that even before our hike; I've heard my mom talk about it.

Yet this is the story we tell. Why do we choose to talk about people sacrificing their lives for their beliefs?

I wonder if I believe in anything so passionately that I would die for it, or at least risk my life to preserve those beliefs. I don't know if I do. Maybe that's something that builds up in people as they keep going and experiencing and living their lives.

Chaya lets us look around before we have to make our harrowing climb back up the thin steps.

"Look," Sammy says. "Birthright Babes, 2003."

"Over here is some group from '75," David says.

"I found one from the 1600s. In Sharpie." Saron points to a group of signatures, and Joshua actually looks.

There's writing along the walls, tour graffiti, mostly in

English. I bet English-speaking tourists are the most likely to believe they have the right to scribble all over an ancient site.

"Should we write something?" Joshua asks. He tries to whisper it, but the cavern basically amplifies everything.

"Yes, let's mess up history with our signatures. We matter more," Saron says flatly. But then she takes out a pen from her bag.

Joshua acts as a lookout—like we might get in trouble doing the thing countless other groups have done—as Saron starts writing.

"We all sign the bottom and then scatter." She says the last part looking directly at Joshua.

I look at her inscription. It says:

Jew Crew

We all sign underneath.

SO MUCH BETTER

"I've named ours Camelot Jones," Max says proudly. He convinced me that, for the sake of pictures and posterity, we needed to go on the camel ride together. *Mom and Dad will love it*, he claimed.

He's still acting weird around me . . . too nice.

"Mine is called Masada Mike. Like our Masada hike but also an homage to male strippers," Saron says.

"Our camel is a stripper?" Sammy asks.

"One with a great film career ahead of him," Saron confirms.

We're back at the Bedouin resort, fed and somewhat caffeinated by instant coffee. Our baseball caps have been replaced by protective helmets.

We've been given some short instructions on how to not be monsters to the camels, and then it's time to actually ride them.

This is sort of like horseback riding, except there are harnesses for two people on each animal; they're hooked up in groups, and there are people in charge of leading us around. So basically, nothing like horseback riding.

Jess is walking alongside us, snapping pictures and meeting her true grandma potential. She says we'll thank her later when we can upload the pictures and/or cherish them forever in nice frames by our bedsides.

"Don't you want to ride too?" I ask.

"No, no. I don't really approve of the way the camels are treated," she says. "I work at an animal rescue center," she explains.

I wonder whether or not I'm awful right now. Should I get off?

Jess adds, "No judgment. The pictures look great."

We're led around a short stretch of desert. I feel slightly ridiculous with the bulky helmet, and it's not exactly the most comfortable of experiences, but we're having fun. I'm on a camel . . . in the desert . . . in Israel . . . on New Year's Day.

When we're done, Chaya gathers us outside our group's tent.

"There is an activity," she says. "Go with a person that you didn't spend much time with."

Which leads to the inevitable scramble. The first person who I lock eyes with is Rivkah. She smiles.

"Team?" she asks.

"Team," I confirm.

Rivkah. We're basically strangers, but I'm curious. I've been thinking about how her brother died. How we're from somewhere so different, yet we've experienced such similar things.

After we form our little teams, Chaya says, "I want you to decide your Jewish life." Jess and David are tasked with handing out laminated worksheets to the group that ask questions like, "Will you raise your kids Jewish?" and "Will you join your local Jewish Community Center?"

"Mazel tov," Chaya says. "You are now married. Look at your partner. You answer questions together, as a pretend family."

We have five minutes to plan out our joint lives, so we jump right in.

"I'd prefer to raise our three beautiful children reform. Or secular," I say. "Holidays?"

"High Holidays, yes. Others?" She shrugs. She's a little unsure with every English word. I feel bad that I can't speak to her in Hebrew.

"Do we live in America or Israel?" I ask.

"Both," she says. "We visit both."

"I like it. We can split the time until the kids are old enough for school; then we'll just live in one and spend summers in the other. We can figure that out later."

We go through the whole list pretty quickly.

"I think we won at married life," I say.

"Yes," she says.

We're silent for a moment.

I play with the laminated paper, curling it on one end. "Rivkah?"

"Yes?"

"I'm sorry about your brother," I say. It feels weak and inadequate.

"I miss him," she says. "But he's here." She puts her hand over her heart. "You miss someone too," she says. And it's not a question. "They're here."

I nod. We don't talk for the rest of the activity. Instead, I stare at the sheet, now slightly curled from my fidgeting. I look at the words without taking in their meaning until Chaya calls us together to share with the group.

After, we have a little time before we need to be on the bus for our ride to Jerusalem. We didn't unpack everything, so it's just making sure we have our day bags ready to go.

The bus still isn't ready, so Jess decides to show off her photos as we sit around a large picnic table, just outside the tent we all slept in last night.

"Joshua and Gabriel, this one has to be my favorite," Jess says, turning her phone toward the boys. It's the two of them making silly faces. Joshua has his hands off the harness, stretched out in the air like he's the star of some stage. Gabriel is clapping his back.

"Oh, I love this one. Classic Gelmont twins," Jess adds, moving the phone toward me.

In the picture, Max is doing this weird hang-ten gesture, and I'm laughing. He has on sunglasses, and I have my head thrown back. It all seems pure.

Maybe I will get it printed out.

The bus is finally ready, so we do our roll call and get on board.

"Mind if I join you?" David asks, pointing to the seat next to me.

I shrug. Buddies can sit together, right?

We have about an hour and a half ride to Jerusalem, and I intend to sleep the whole time. "I don't plan to be chatty," I warn.

"I certainly hope not. This is my nap time."

"I forgot you're four."

"Almost four. Three and eleven-twelfths," he clarifies.

"Complicated math for your age."

"My mom says I'm advanced." He sits down.

"You snore?" I ask.

"Loud as a train. Drool?"

"Absolute faucet."

"Quite the pair," he says.

We're quiet for a while but in a comfortable sort of way. I don't know exactly when I fell asleep, but I wake up with my head resting on his shoulder, and it's not bad.

TRADITION

We're in Jerusalem now, which feels big. This is it: the setting of all those sacred stories, the place we are supposed to pray for, to make a pilgrimage to. Even at a Jewish wedding, you step on a glass before the mazel tovs to remember the destruction of the Temple in Jerusalem.

The bus stops in front of the nicest hotel yet, big and fancy-looking. Chaya said that there's even a pool. *A pool.*

Everything is a little bittersweet, though, because we have to say goodbye to the Israelis.

"Stay in touch," Saron demands, hugging Rivkah. "And we'll see you in a few months. I'm going to force you to eat so much American junk food; it's going to be the best."

"Yes," Rivkah says. "Very excited."

She turns to me. "Tally," she starts.

"It was lovely raising our three children," I say. "We really did have a great life together."

She laughs. "You are, eh"—she waves her hand as though she is trying to think of the correct English word—"funny." We follow each other on Instagram before she leaves.

After we say our goodbyes, we walk into the hotel. While the hotel in Tel Aviv felt cramped, in a boutique, metropolitan sort of way, this feels grand and sprawling. There's room to move here. We're settled into a section of the lobby with red-and-gold couches and a glass coffee table, waiting to hear our room assignments and the plan for the rest of the night.

"Think we'll be together again?" I ask Saron.

"Oh, definitely," she says. "Jess is my secret agent, infiltrating the room-assignment system from the inside."

She's right; Saron, Sammy, and I end up in a room together. There's more space here than our last room. Saron immediately declares it an ideal size for hosting.

"Hosting what exactly?" I ask, plopping onto my bed. I'm in the middle of the three this time. My suitcase is already open by my feet so I can change into clothes that aren't covered in remnants of Masada and don't smell like camel.

Saron shrugs, waving a dismissive hand. "We'll see where the night takes us."

This night in particular is Shabbat, so I have to think Saron won't get too far in any schemes.

When I was little, we used to celebrate Shabbat every Friday. We even had a tzedakah box for collecting money for charities, which we used before we lit the candles and blessed the challah. After the blessings, it was basically just a family dinner with a phones-off rule.

Mom always ended up running the whole thing, which seemed kind of silly, since she's Catholic. Eventually we stopped. I guess we just got busy. I had play practices and Max started his short-lived band.

I miss Shabbat sometimes. I miss sitting around for our technology-free family dinner, waving our hands by the light of the candles and saying the blessing, so familiar that I could recite it without thought.

I wonder if it will feel the same way tonight.

There's some time before we have to meet up with the group, and Saron calls first shower.

"I smell like camel," she says. She unbuttons her pants while she's still standing by her bed.

I turn away.

"I have the same parts, Tally Mark," Saron says. I can hear the judgment, like I failed some kind of test because I looked away.

"I'm just giving you some privacy," I say.

She lets out a little huff of breath like I just said something amusing. "Very considerate but unnecessary."

From the side of my eye, I see her walk past me on the way to the bathroom, wearing nothing but a T-shirt and underwear.

I stare very carefully at the duvet on my bed until I hear the door close.

Is it wrong that I've been changing in the bathroom? Is it wrong that I feel weird around people when they aren't fully dressed? Does that make me a prude?

I've thought about myself as a prude before. I can't escape it. Basically everything I watch is sex- and body-positive, but it's often in a way that veers in this direction where I feel like I should be ashamed by my lack of experience.

My mind wanders to David. The image of our kiss pops into my head even though I really don't want to think about it. Does my reaction prove that I'm a prude?

No, I can't think about that right now. I get off my bed and grab some clean clothes from my suitcase. I wait until I can use the bathroom to change.

Once all of us are ready, we go to the meeting place. The whole group gathers in a conference room, which feels like a weird place to bring in Shabbat. There's a whiteboard at one end and a group of chairs organized in a circle. I think Jess and David were tasked with setting this up, because David is moving the last chair as we walk in, and Jess is writing Shabbat Shalom on the board in her flowing script.

We take our seats and Chaya starts. She lights the candles at a small table in front of the whiteboard, then makes circular motions with her hands, bringing the light to her face. She puts her hands over her eyes. We all say the prayer together. Baruch atah, Adonai, Eloheinu, melech haolam, asher kid'shanu b'mitzvotav, v'tzivanu l'hadlik ner shel Shabbat. The words are so familiar, so comfortable.

I feel at home.

I remember the special challah Dad would pick up from the bakery in Brookline and the candlestick holders Max and I made when we were little and still went to Hebrew school. I miss it. I didn't really care before—if anything, I was indifferent to mildly annoyed—but as we pass around the bread and say the blessings, I feel guilty that we ever stopped.

I wonder if Mom and Dad would be okay with bringing back our weekly Shabbat dinner.

"Eat, sleep," Chaya says as a dismissal. "Do as you wish. We will have a later morning, ten in the lobby. Now is the time of rest."

WHY WE BUILD THE WALL

I'm working on a new song when Joshua walks into the hotel room.

"I've been thinking," he starts, unprompted, "that we need to do something for the banner."

I curse. "How the hell did you get in here?"

"Saron told me she'd leave the door open," he says dismissively, sitting down at the edge of my bed. Gabriel walks into the room behind him. "Now, the banner."

"One-track mind," Gabriel explains. "He knows not what he does."

Saron, lying on her own bed, looks up. She puts down her sketch pad on the bedside table. "Sorry," she says to me. "I did tell him to come in. I didn't tell him to come in ranting about an inanimate object, but . . ."

"Not just any inanimate object—we're talking about the banner here," Joshua corrects. "I've realized that we need to do something big. Something exciting! Something that will truly honor the magic of the banner!"

"And what's that exactly?" Saron asks.

"I haven't decided yet!" Joshua says with the same emphasis and momentum as he would have if he were announcing a concrete plan.

Saron puts her hands over her eyes like she's trying to massage away a particularly nasty headache.

"Any ideas?" Gabriel asks, still standing near the door.

"Well, since it's New Year's Day, I was thinking maybe we could find some kind of fireworks show. Do you think they'll still have those? Or would that have been last night? Wait, are you allowed to set off fireworks on Shabbat?" Joshua asks.

I sigh. This might take some time. Some loud time. Some loud, non-writing time.

"I'll be right back," I say, picking up my phone and my notebook. I slide my key card off the nightstand and slip it into my back pocket.

"Take me with you," Saron says.

"You invited him here; you need to live with your mistakes," I say.

I walk out of the room. We're at the far end of the hallway, away from the elevators. I think about going to the lobby or down to the dining room, but instead I set up outside the room, sliding down the navy wall to sit on the faded blue carpet.

I'm working on a song inspired by Shabbat, playing

around with the term "day of rest." You can do a lot with it. Stressed, addressed, messed. Blessed.

The page in my notebook looks messy, filled with crossed-out lines and arrows. I have a note on the side that just says: *tap number?* At this point, the lyrics all look like gibberish. I need to take a break.

I decide to FaceTime my parents.

"Happy New Year," I say when my mom picks up.

"A little late to the game," Mom says. I can see her take a sip of her tea, then place it back down out of view of the camera. She's sitting on our living room couch, a knit throw blanket wrapped around her shoulders.

"Happy it's the first day of the New Year and we didn't have Wi-Fi last night because we were sleeping in the desert," I try again.

"Happy New Year!" Dad calls out from off-screen.

"Your father is making pancakes," Mom explains. "Also, I know you've had access to Wi-Fi for at least a couple of hours; I already talked to your brother."

"You talked to Max?" I ask.

"Of course, he's been calling every day to check in," Mom says. "Which is better than *some people* have been doing," she adds pointedly.

This shouldn't be a competition, but it certainly feels like one. "What has he been saying?" I ask.

"That you two went to the Dead Sea and hiked Masada. Haven't been to the Western Wall yet, even though, if I were organizing this trip, it would have been one of the first things you saw." She takes another sip of tea.

I sigh.

"He also mentioned that you had a rough night," she finishes.

I shift in my spot, back a little straighter now. "He said what?"

"Tally, he was just worried." She pauses. "Do you want to talk about what happened?"

"Nothing happened," I say.

"This isn't a fight. We all just want to help you."

"I don't need help," I say sharply. I've done everything right. I've been there for Max; I've gotten great grades. I already got into college. I'm not the one who needs help. "I'm fine."

"You don't need to be fine right now. I'm still not fine," she says. "Catherine was like another child."

"I don't want to talk about it," I say.

"But, Tally, at some point you're going to have to," she says. She holds her mug, fingers wrapped around the ceramic. I can tell it's warm from the thin waft of steam rising from the cup. "You know," she continues, "your brother started to see Dr. Rosen. I can schedule an appointment for you when you get back."

Another thing he didn't tell me. "I don't need that," I say.

"But it's an option." She puts down her mug without taking a sip. "You should go have fun. Enjoy your trip."

"I have been," I say.

"I know, baby. I love you," she adds.

She hangs up.

I sit there, back against the wall, staring at a bit of carpet opposite from me that's pulling up at the edges.

I don't need therapy.

Do I?

This isn't the first time I've talked about therapy with my parents. Mom is big on making your own choices with your mental-health journey. I guess I've been really good at pretending like I can take care of things myself, an image I crafted even before Cat died.

There are a thousand reasons. I like control, I hate asking for help, I don't want to admit that my anxiety has gone beyond home remedies. I'm embarrassed that I can't fix myself.

The facade was just easier.

Then Max ruined it all by telling on me.

There's this childish anger that bubbles up around the thought. He snitched. Why did he do that? It's not like I called up our parents to say I caught him crying the other night.

We're supposed to be a team, and he betrayed me.

I start to get angry about other things: the fact that he lied to our friends on the trip about why I left the club, how clingy he's been since my panic attack. He's treating me like I'm breakable, like I might fall apart at any moment. And worse, he's making *other* people worry about me too.

Suddenly, it's too much. I gather my things and head toward his hotel room, my feet pounding down the hallway.

If he thinks *I'm* the one people need to be worried about, then fine.

I'll give him something to worry about.

WHAT I DID FOR LOVE

"Max," I yell, banging my fist on his door. "Max!"

He opens the door and steps back into the room. "You can come in; my roommates are at the pool. What's up?" He's not even looking at me. He walks over to his bed and sits up against the pillows, his eyes on his phone.

I follow, stopping near the end of his bed. "I just talked to Mom. What the hell?"

He puts down his phone. "Is everything okay?"

"No," I say. "Nothing is okay. You told Mom I had a panic attack."

He sighs. "Tal, come on. Of course I told Mom and Dad. They asked me about the trip and how you were doing. Was I supposed to lie?"

"Yes. You're supposed to be on my team."

"What team, Tally? You've been so closed off and weird. For months. I've barely been able to talk to you; you keep shutting down anything that comes anywhere near real human emotions."

"So, what? That makes it okay? You've been basically spying on me," I yell. "You know Mom asked *me* to keep an eye on *you*."

"Yeah, and she asked me to do the same thing. We've all been worried about you since Cat died." His voice sounds so sincere that it's verging on condescending.

"That's ridiculous," I say. "I'm fine."

"You're not even a little fine," Max says. "You're acting like you've moved on completely. You can't just move on from your best friend."

"Yes. Yes, I can," I say. Because I'm angry. I'm angry with Max for telling on me; I'm angry with Cat for being gone. "She made the choices she did. She got in that car; she drove. And then she almost killed you. Maybe she succeeded—with how you've been acting, it's like the *real* you disappeared."

"What are you talking about?" he asks.

"Don't pretend like you don't know what I mean. You're the one who's been depressed. You're the one who skipped school and missed the early application deadline, which left *me* the job of trying to salvage our senior year. I'm the one who has been trying to fix you!"

"*Fix me?* Are you kidding me right now?"

"I've been busting my butt trying to make you better. Do you know how hard it's been? You just kept on being sad, no matter what I did. Then the moment you start feeling a little better, you turn this on me?"

I probably should stop there, but I'm going on anger-fueled momentum now, so I continue. "I'm the one who got us on this trip. I'm the one who got you to socialize. I'm the one who set you up with Sammy."

He goes still. "You did *what*?"

"Set you up with Sammy," I continue. "It's not like it's been easy; Saron and I have been trying for days to make this happen."

His voice drops. "You dragged other people into this?"

"Yes! Because you were useless by yourself. The street-art-tour picture, losing you guys in the market. That was us. That was me. It clearly worked; I know you kissed Sammy. Saron told me."

"And I'm the one spying on you. Right." He folds his arms against his chest. "That meant nothing. It was a New Year's kiss with a girl I barely know."

"Kisses don't mean nothing," I say.

He rolls his eyes.

In this moment, I really hate my brother. I've spent so long thinking about how to help him through a tough time, and he turns around and does this. Everything he is saying makes me feel like I'm small and naive. It makes me feel like he's trying to discredit all the worry and care I put into trying to help him.

"I've been working so hard to make you happy," I say at last.

"No, Tally," he says, his voice laced with so much venom that I flinch. "You're just being unnecessarily anxious. You've been working hard to *manipulate* me." He shakes his head. "But I don't need fixing. All I need is for you to get the hell out of here."

"I'm already leaving," I growl. "I don't even want to *look* at you!"

"Good," he says.

"Good!" I yell back. Then I head to his door and slam it on my way out.

He can't be angry with me if I'm angry with him first. I haven't done a single thing wrong. Not. A. Single. Thing.

I storm back to my room, ready to collapse on my bed or maybe scream into a pillow like it's an endless void.

Instead, I walk in to find a very confusing scene.

"I'm just not sure if this is a glamour look," Joshua says from where he's sitting cross-legged on Saron's bed. "Have you put on makeup before?"

"Of course I have; you're just being squirmy," Saron says. She puts down her eyeliner. "Tally Mark, you're back."

"You can get started on Gabriel's makeup," Joshua says.

"I don't remember agreeing to anything," Gabriel responds.

Joshua ignores that. "We're doing a fashion show. With the banner. It's going to be stunning."

"He means hilarious," Saron corrects.

I can't deal with any of this right now. "I'm going to take a shower," I say, then walk into the bathroom and close the door.

I don't let myself cry until I'm under the water.

WHAT COMES NEXT?

I'm staring at Max from across the dining room, my hand gripped tightly around my coffee cup. Joshua and Gabriel are sitting with him. They're laughing.

They're sitting together and laughing.

Without me.

Which would be fine if Max hadn't been so pointed about it. If he hadn't taken his plate and walked right past me. If I hadn't seen him stop Joshua and Gabriel, waving them over to his table.

He doesn't need my help; he made that clear. Well, I don't need his either. I have friends on this trip. Like Saron, who is still asleep, and Sammy, who went to the gym.

I'll be fine alone.

I would have continued to be fine sitting alone in the dining room even if David didn't sit down across from me. Since our talk, I actually feel good being around him. It's the lack of pressure, I think.

"I hear there's an omelet station," he starts.

"Go on," I say.

"Legend tells of a place where the eggs are cracked, the yolk mixed, the ingredients added. Many have searched and many have failed to find this magnificent—"

Such. A. Dork.

I cut him off. "Adventure?"

"Adventure." He nods.

I don't know why there would be a food station outside, but that's the only clue David has for our egg hunt. After a quick check, we find out that it is indeed not inside the dining area, so we'll have to check outside. The only problem is that we can't figure out how to get there.

"We don't have to go up the stairs, do we? That would be ridiculous. Would that be ridiculous?" he asks.

"I think I saw a door out if you go through the gym, but that's on the other side of the building."

"We could check the pool. There could be a *bottom of the pool Atlantis secret egg station*. Om-lantis."

We end up walking through the gym to get to the pool. Sammy isn't there anymore; she must be back in our room. I get a couple of frowns for walking past the old-as-the-Torah ellipticals with my coffee.

David leans down next to the pool, and if I were just a little meaner, I would definitely push him in. "Nothing." He runs a hand through the water. "I see nothing."

Is it wrong that I think that's cute? I'm not supposed to think anything David does is cute because we are just friends, right?

I look away from him, back toward the dining room. We should probably admit defeat, I think. Which is naturally when I see it.

I tap David's shoulder. "Look."

I point to the omelet station, just past the pool.

"Om-lantis!" he says.

We order, and the food looks delicious. We're about to take our breakfast back inside when we see a curtain get pushed aside to reveal the dining area.

"Where have you two been?" Saron asks, walking up to the omelet station.

"We got . . . turned around," I say. Then I whisper to David, "The door was right there?"

"Not our fault they hid it," he quietly assures me.

We wait for Saron to get her food and then head back into the dining area to finish breakfast together.

Take that, Max. At least some people like me.

———

Our bus driver has the day off for Shabbat, so our morning plan is to walk as a group to the Israel Museum.

Saron is practically buzzing the closer we get. ". . . and the design of the Shrine of the Book? It's a dome and also sort of like a fountain and then it's across from a black wall, which is supposed to symbolize light versus the darkness and sure the whole white versus black thing is shady but they're trying to be all biblical and did I mention the Dead Sea Scrolls are actually inside? *The* Dead Sea Scrolls. Don't even get me started on the art wing. The contemporary collection is going to put me in a state of literal ecstasy. And the . . ."

I'm not completely sure whether she is going to stop talking the entire time that we're walking to the museum.

Max is still avoiding me. He stays near the back of the group our whole walk over. I try testing it, just to see, slowing down so I get closer to where he is in the group. He starts walking faster.

Childish, that's what it is. He's being childish.

I don't need this.

Once we get to the museum, Chaya gives us a meeting time and place and then dismisses us to go look through the galleries.

"Where's your brother?" Saron asks.

He bolted so he didn't have to spend time with me, that's what happened, but I can't say that to Saron.

I shrug. "Must have already gone inside."

"His loss; I'm an amazing museum tour guide. You're about to learn so much," she says excitedly. She starts walking toward the Shrine of the Book.

Sammy and I follow.

We walk down a set of stairs into a dark exhibit. Honestly, it feels less like a museum and more like a scene out of some high-stakes adventure movie. I'm expecting a giant boulder to come rolling over toward us at any moment. I'm not sure what we're looking for, but Saron is in the lead, so I follow.

We continue on into a curved room with textured, striped

walls. It's dimly lit, so the whole room looks softly muted and yellow, like it was passed over with a filter. We see the scrolls in the center of the room inside a big Torah-shaped glass structure. We can only see part of the display from here, raised above our heads. The scrolls are wrapped in a circle, so we'll need to walk the circumference to see the full display. There are other pieces of parchment around the room in smaller, rectangular cases.

"When the scrolls were discovered, some of them were in bad shape. The ones they could identify were writings from different Judaic sects, works that weren't canonized in the bible, or pieces of ancient Hebrew scripture. That right there—" Saron points. "Ancient scripture."

Ancient scripture.

I imagine my mom standing here, excitedly gushing over the importance of these pieces of weathered paper and the words inscribed on them. They look too worn to be so important.

We walk over to take a closer look, going up a set of winding stairs. We pass the other cases because Saron is on a mission.

"Can you translate any of it?" I ask.

"Maybe a few words?" Saron squints at the small text. "Not all of it is in Hebrew. I think there's Aramaic and Greek in there too."

We stare at the display for a few minutes, walking around the circular structure. Saron finds the words "land" and "wash."

Sammy takes out her phone. "Is it sacrilegious to post this online?" she asks.

We don't get a chance to answer because she is very quickly yelled at by an old guard. "No photos!" he says in an exasperated sort of way, like he has to say this a million times a day.

"We're so sorry," Saron says to the guard. She goes back to looking at the scrolls, looping around the side. When she comes back, she leans closer to us and whispers, "That's how it's done." I don't know what she's talking about until I look down and see her phone, angled up by her waist. It's open to a photo of the scrolls.

"Saron, he just told us not to do that," I whisper.

Saron shakes her head, like this is just another case of my rule-following nature getting in the way. "We had this guest speaker in one of my art classes," she says, "a curator. She said as long as you don't use the flash, you're fine. They just want to up the sales at the gift store."

After we leave the Shrine of the Book, Saron heads us straight to the main building of the museum. We walk past the sections on archeology and Jewish culture, going right to the modern-art section.

". . . don't even get me started on Gertrude Stein. She basically invented Picasso, invited all these people to her personal home showings so they had to like it all. But wilder, she was a Jewish lesbian in German-occupied France, and no one touched her because she was practically made of money and also kind of a Nazi sympathizer? How does that even make sense? Did you hear the Jewish lesbian part? And Duchamp, just wild. So this one time he took a urinal and . . ."

She barely stops to breathe until we see my brother. He's standing in the Impressionist section in front of a painting by Monet, *Water Lilies.*

Cat's favorite. She had a framed print on the wall above her bed.

"There you are," Saron says, like we were looking for him this whole time. "I'm about to change all of your lives."

He raises an eyebrow.

"I'm basically an art expert, come on," she says.

"You guys go ahead," he says.

"What? So you can stay in front of *that*?" Saron says, waving toward the water lilies. "You know there are, like, hundreds of those. You can see them in basically any museum."

Cat liked that. She said that it made the experience universal. *You can travel the world and we're all admiring the same things: Degas and his dancers, the water lilies, that statue of the word "love." We're all the same, on a certain level.*

I look at the brushstrokes, thick and clear from this close up. I can't see the whole painting, though, because my brother is blocking the way.

"You don't have to come," I say.

Max narrows his eyes. "Why? Does that go against your *plans*?"

I tense my shoulders. *What's the worst thing that could happen?* I try to comfort myself.

He turns to Sammy and Saron, looking away from the

painting. "You know, this was Cat's favorite painting. Tally's told you guys about Cat, right?" Before they can say anything, he continues. "She was Tally's best friend. She died last summer in a car accident. Drunk driving, actually. I was in the car too."

What's the worst thing that could happen? This.

I can't move. I think I might throw up all over myself because I can't move a single muscle and my stomach feels incurably sick.

"Oh, I'm so sorry; I had no idea," Sammy says.

"Neither did I," Saron adds. I think she's going to call me a liar for leaving that out when I told her about the car accident, but she doesn't say anything else.

There's a silence so thick, I can feel it in the air.

Max is the first to speak. "I think I will tag along," he says. "Let's move on. You want to *move on*, right, Tally?"

I don't answer immediately because I know what he's *really* saying is that I'm broken and manipulative and a liar. He wants Saron to know the truth—that she got caught up in my web of lies and should never talk to me again. He wants Sammy to know all about how we essentially pimped her out. He wants everyone to be mad at me, to yell at me, to pity me—

I was helping him. That was all I was doing. I don't deserve any of this.

"Go ahead—I'll catch up with you."

"You sure?" Saron asks. Her voice is soft and hesitant. I don't hear any hate in her words, but I can sense the pity.

"Yeah, I just need a moment. I'll be right behind you."

I know this is a lie. I think they know too, but they still

walk ahead. I can hear Saron talking about Cubism from the other room.

I turn in the opposite direction, find the nearest bathroom, and lock myself in a stall. I feel so nauseous that I actually lean over the toilet, but nothing happens.

Nothing happened when Max told them about Cat, not really. They just felt bad for me, sorry for something they could never understand. I should have known that's all that would happen because no one knows how to respond to death. There's no good response. There's nothing a person can say to fix things, since there is no fix.

I leave the bathroom. I need to clear my head, so I decide to walk aimlessly through the galleries we rushed past on the way to the modern-art section. There are religious objects and re-creations of temples, a set of endless rooms with endless objects that don't really register.

A painting catches my eye, and I stop. I didn't even realize I had looped back to the art galleries.

I look at the pale pinks and greens and blues, cut through with white for the light reflected on the painted water.

"Monet's *Water Lilies*. Did you know he made hundreds of them?" asks a voice right behind me.

It's David. I had no idea he was even in the gallery, let alone looking at the same painting.

"I heard there's a room in Paris where you can twirl around and around and see nothing but water lilies," I say, turning my focus back to the painting.

"You can even visit his house, where he worked on the series. It's in some village in France," David adds.

"I'll go for my next trip," I say.

"Great idea."

I think that maybe I should walk away and continue my lonely, aimless journey through the museum. That's definitely what I should do. I don't deserve to spend time with anyone else.

I study the painting quietly, remembering the way it looked hanging by her bed. It wasn't the same exact one; hers had more vibrant shades of green and blue. There's still something so familiar about the one here. I think about Cat's words, how she called it *universal*.

This feels universal.

I turn to David. "Want to see a sculpture? They have one of those Love ones, you know, where the word *is* the statue, but here it's in Hebrew." Another of Cat's favorites.

"I'm sold," he says.

"I really didn't do much selling," I say.

"Fine, then I'm out. You need to work a little harder to get me to follow your wild plans, you know; maybe I already had something that I—"

"Come on." I roll my eyes. I push his arm a little to get him going and then lead the way.

Or try to lead the way. I get us outside, but then I'm lost.

"Is there a map?" I ask. I take out the museum brochure to see if I can find anything to help us. I feel like I've reached peak tourist.

David stands behind me, craning his neck down, trying

to read along. "A map to Love? Never," he says with mock seriousness.

"You're the worst," I say flatly, but then I smile.

We look together, away from the main section of the museum, back past the Shrine of the Book. It's like Om-lantis, part two. I'm worried we're not going to find the statue, since we're supposed to meet up with everyone in about ten minutes by the big re-creation of old Jerusalem.

We turn a corner, and it's right in front of us. *Love, Ahava.* The statue is by a ledge, but we're safely on the other side. Behind it, we can see sections of Jerusalem, buildings small in the distance.

We don't say anything for a while. We just look at the statue, its weathered steel, tall against the backdrop of the city and the cloudless blue sky. *Ahava, Love.* Rusted and old and huge and universal.

Then David turns to me, hand raised expectantly. "We found it," he says.

"We found it," I say and give him a high five.

This high five feels far more intimate than when we kissed. I like it; I really do. I like everything about spending time with David, from trying to find the omelet station to getting lost in this museum to sleeping on the bus with my head on his shoulder.

All those things aren't supposed to feel more intimate than kissing.

I wonder if anyone else in the entire universe has ever felt this confused before.

I take one last look at the statue of Love, then the two of us leave to find the group so we can walk back to the hotel.

—————

After Havdalah, the closing of Shabbat, Chaya announces that we're going to walk to the Jerusalem shuk.

I stop Max as the group is walking out of the conference room we just used for our meeting. "I'm not going," I say. "So you don't have to worry about bullying me in front of our friends."

"Bullying. Right." His voice is quiet, but there's an unmistakable edge. "That's what I was doing. I forgot telling the truth counts as bullying; how silly of me."

He's such a jerk.

"Well, you don't have to worry," I continue. "I'm tapping out; you take tonight."

"Oh, that's so generous of you," he says mockingly.

"It is," I say back.

Most of the group has already filtered out of the room, the last few stragglers standing by the door.

"You know what, you take tonight. I'm not in the mood for forced socialization."

"You know it wasn't like that," I say.

"Sure."

"Well, we both shouldn't back out," I add.

"You go. Pretend everything is fine; it's what you do best."

I clench my fists. "Fine. Then I'm going tonight."

"Good."

"Great."

I want to punch him.

Instead, I catch up to Saron.

"Everything okay?" she asks, slowing down. "Thought we lost you."

"Oh, it's nothing," I say. "Had to check in with Max. He has a headache; he's staying behind to rest."

"Must run in the family," she says.

I frown, then remember the lie he told about me that night after the club. *Great.*

I think about coming up with another excuse, but Saron moves on.

"About earlier," she starts.

Oh no. "We don't have to . . ."

She doesn't stop talking. "It's fine that you didn't tell me. I know this whole experience has thrown us together, and we really just met, you know, in the grand scheme of things. I just wanted to say that I can be a person you talk to, if that's something you need. Or the person who distracts you or sets you up with someone or stands around being ridiculously good-looking to make you feel better." She cracks a smile at her last suggestion. "Whatever you need, I'm here."

Unlike when we were at the museum, I don't hear any pity in her words. I was so worried that everything would change if the truth got out. I was worried that Saron would hate me, since I told her about the car crash but left out the part about Cat. I still think that makes me a monster, but she isn't running and hiding.

I'm here. I'm not sure I can articulate how much that means to me.

I nod.

"Now, hurry up—we don't want to get lost," she says.

We join the rest of the group and head out into the city.

UNRULY HEART

Chaya reins us in before we get to the market. "I have an announcement. I was working hard to get this permission and just found out the answer is yes." She takes a deep breath and looks over at Jess. Jess nods reassuringly, a small smile on her face. "Tomorrow is Jerusalem Pride. It's not like what you might think of Pride. The *oooh yeah wild*, that is for Tel Aviv. Here it's about respect. Here is a city of religion but also, we try, a city of love.

"I work with kids when I'm not doing this. Some were sent out of their homes, others told they are not part of their family, because of who they are. Who they love. This is who I work with. This is for them.

"I must say, some years ago, a thing happened. At the Pride, as people were walking, a young girl was killed. She was killed by an Orthodox man. She was sixteen.

"I say this for the truth. This happened. Tomorrow, there

will be much security, but if you feel any worry, I understand. So Pride tomorrow, we can go. We got permission, but it's up to you. Something to think about. That is for tomorrow; tonight we have food. Meet here at—" She pauses and looks at her watch. "Nine. We will walk back together." She pauses and looks at us. "Go, go. If you want recommendations for food, I'll stay here for some minutes. Go."

"We're all going tomorrow," Saron says in a matter-of-fact tone.

I want to say "yes, definitely," but my brain keeps thinking that it's too dangerous. Someone was *murdered*.

A sixteen-year-old died at a peaceful Pride march. A girl who was younger than I am. The danger level builds in my head. There will be a crowd, first of all, and you never know who could be in a crowd. Then there's the fact that it's Pride.

Shouldn't this be something I support no matter what? Because I do support Pride. I support love, and love is love is love no matter what form it comes in.

Not that it applies to me, because I'll never find love and I'm broken and wrong, of course.

"I'm going," says Joshua.

Gabriel nods.

I don't say anything. I'm probably going to go. I know that I'm probably going to go.

Which is why I'm relieved when Saron changes the subject.

"I'm so excited that we're all focused on tomorrow, but my stomach thinks you all are evil. I need sustenance *now*," she says.

"I could really go for some jachnun. There's a place close by, I think," Sammy says.

"Some what?" Saron asks.

"Jachnun. It's a Yemenite dish, basically a thin pastry that you can add stuff into. It's good."

"I've had it before," Gabriel says. "Delicious."

Sammy has an international phone plan, so she takes out her phone and looks up the place. It's really close. We wind our way past the shuk and down a side street.

We arrive at the small shop with tables scattered around just outside the entrance. Inside, there's a counter set up with all the food you can add to the jachnun, like cucumber and eggplant. To be honest, it looks extremely similar to a falafel place.

"What am I supposed to put in this?" I ask.

"I'm getting one roll with an egg. And tomatoes. Oh, there's eggplant too," Sammy says, her eyes focused on the counter of food.

I wait until everyone else has ordered to get mine and then join them all at the table. Or rather, the group of tables they have smooshed together to form one mega table. We're just the kind of customers businesses love.

"Tattoos are out for tonight," Joshua dramatically announces, walking over to us from outside the shop and plopping down on the seat next to mine. "Apparently, the nearest place doesn't have any reservations open, and technically it's not even within our boundaries."

"Rough," Gabriel says.

"I don't know, man; I thought this would be easier. Don't

people get drunk all the time and accidentally get tatted up? We have a full-fledged plan. We should be rewarded for this."

"Tattoos?" I ask.

"To honor the banner," Saron explains. "It was my idea." She has a mischievous look on her face.

"Isn't that, like . . . distinctly against Jewish customs?" I ask.

"That's so dated." Saron waves it off. "Plus, it would have been extremely funny if I convinced Joshua to get a #IVEGOTCHUTZPAH tramp stamp."

I'm not sure if Joshua hears her, because he doesn't respond. Instead, he looks dejectedly at his food. "We need to figure out something else. Need to. We're almost out of time," he says quietly, as though he is talking only to himself.

He seems bummed out for the rest of the meal. Gabriel claps him reassuringly on the back a few times, and he looks over and says, "I know, man. Thanks."

There are a couple of shops that are open for the post-Shabbat crowd. We do a little bit of window-shopping before we have to meet up with the group.

It's as we're window-shopping that Joshua finds the boxers.

"Israeli flag boxers," he says in awe, holding up the plastic package they come in. "This. This could be the answer."

"The answer to what?" Saron asks.

"To the banner problem," he declares.

"I'm not buying boxers," Saron says.

"I'll get them for everyone! I'm feeling generous. Why else have I babysat for the last two years?"

"Because it's your job," Gabriel says.

"So you would have your own money," I offer.

"No," Joshua says, "it was definitely all leading up to this moment. Everything has a purpose."

He buys the whole stock of boxers without counting them and then dramatically hands them out like some creepy Hanukkah Harry.

He looks so happy, though.

We continue on to meet the group, each holding a pair of Israeli flag boxers.

"David! Jess!" Joshua yells out. They're waiting down the street at the meeting point. "I bought you boxers!"

I look over at Saron. "Did he say how this fixes the banner problem?" I ask.

She shakes her head. "I think it's best not to ask questions when you don't want to hear the answer."

So we continue walking over to join the group without further explanation.

$$\Rightarrow \quad \text{———} \quad \Leftarrow$$

Knock. Knock, knock, knock. Knock.

I look up from my notebook. "Did you guys invite someone over?"

Sammy shakes her head, placing her open book on her chest to hold her spot. Saron gets up from her bed without answering. She has a big grin on her face as she opens the door.

The first thing I see through the door is a bottle of Israeli wine. "Surprise!" Jess says, walking in. "Guess who's off the clock!"

"It's fun Jess!" Saron says, clapping excitedly.

Jess laughs. "It's not like there are two versions of me. Working me is still fun."

"Sure," Saron says.

"You'll just be disappointed," Jess says. "Alcohol barely affects me."

After about a glass, she's changed her tune.

"I lied! You fools, I'm a total lightweight! I bet you feel really ridiculous now."

Saron looks absolutely gleeful. She sits cross-legged on the bed, facing Jess. "I feel like we should make the most of this. Play Truth or Dare or something."

"Daaaaare," Jess calls out.

"Put on your own makeup without a mirror. No phone either!" Saron adds.

"Done." Jess heads into the bathroom, grabs the makeup Saron and I told her we left on the counter, and walks back out. "I'm going to look so good," she says, sitting on the floor with the makeup spread out in front of her. She promptly gets lipstick on her chin.

"Next," Saron says. "Sammy, announce on the social media of your choosing that you're engaged."

"Funny how I didn't choose Dare," she says.

"You have to get the Dares out of the way," Saron says. "It loosens you up for Truth."

By the time we transition to Truth, Jess looks like a clown, Saron has her bra on over her shirt, and I'm allowed to speak only if I use a Valley girl accent.

"All right," Saron starts. "Did you hook up with Shira?" she asks Jess. "You definitely thought she was cute."

Jess snorts. "No way, I'd never cheat on Chaya."

"What?" Saron looks like her entire world has just changed. "How did I not know about this?"

"'Cause I'm stealthy . . . like a love spy." Jess giggles into her wine, which she poured into a glass cup in our hotel room that I think the management intended for water.

Saron sighs. "The gays are really winning this trip. We've got Joshua and Gabriel, who are basically soul mates. Apparently, Jess and Chaya. What do the straights have? Nothing substantial," Saron says.

"Oh, are you straight?" Sammy asks.

"I'm not a labels person," Saron says. "It was more of a general observation on our heteronormative failings."

I pause. This feels like an opening. David and I are friends now. Just buddies. I don't know why I freaked out, and I don't think I really want to talk about that part, but I apparently can't stop myself from talking.

"So, I, like . . . totally . . . uh." I drop the exaggerated tone. "This boy kissed me," I say quickly.

"Ohmygawd, you and David kissed?" Saron asks. "I didn't even do anything to set you two up yet."

Yet? Was this something she had planned?

I really hope it wasn't, because I'm still working out all my feelings and that would be supremely unhelpful, harmful even.

Is this how Max felt when I told him I set him up?

I don't have time to linger on that, because everyone keeps talking.

"That is super against the rules," Jess says, using her glass for emphasis. A bit of wine splashes out of her cup and onto the floor.

"You literally just told us you're dating our tour leader," Saron points out. Jess just waves that off. "Sorry, babe, continue."

"It was the night we went to the club in Tel Aviv—"

"And it took you this long to— Never mind, I'll stop, keep going."

I rub the bead on my fidget ring. "I don't know. I freaked out. I just felt like I wasn't really there, you know? Like I was watching it all? And I don't know, maybe I'm weird, but I think I can't actually tell if I even find him attractive. Like, what is attraction even?"

Saron sits up. She asks, "Have you ever been attracted to anyone?"

"I mean, I guess I've had crushes before, but nothing has really happened." Fidgeting with the bead on my ring isn't enough now. I take my hair out of my ponytail, run my fingers through it. Put it back up again.

"What do you find sexy?" Saron asks.

I don't know how to answer that, because what is sexy? Like, I can understand the hot factor of certain actors, but I would never actually want to do anything with them. Apparently, I wouldn't even want to do anything with the kind boy who wanted to kiss me. Then there's the whole touch thing.

Why did I act that way over the whole touch thing? In the abstract, I think maybe I could like it all someday, with the right person. I don't know who that right person would be. I don't know if anyone else has ever felt this way.

But how do you say any of that out loud?

"I like it when a couple gets together in a movie." It's the only thing I can grasp that seems remotely normal enough to say out loud. "I like the whole relationship, if it's done well. How you can see how they really care for each other and all the emotions and love that build up to them finally, I don't know, kissing."

"Tally, have you considered—and this is just an idea, okay?—that you might be demisexual?" Saron asks.

Which, like, no I have not considered that, because I don't know what that means. "Um?"

"Demisexual," Saron continues. "It means you don't experience sexual attraction unless you form a strong emotional attachment to someone. My cousin is demisexual. And—wait, I think I read an article about it once; give me a second." She reaches over to grab her phone, placed on the nightstand between our beds.

"Okay, okay," she says without taking her eyes off her phone. Her fingers are moving quickly, typing. "Have your past relationships all started as friendships?" she asks, reading off the screen.

"Well, I haven't had a past relationship," I say. "But I think that's probably better for me. To know someone first."

"Let's put that in the yes category," Jess says. She's

climbed onto the bed behind Saron, reading over her shoulder.

"Do your crushes seem really important? Like, it's a big deal just to have a crush," Saron asks.

"Yeah," I say quietly.

"Oh, let me read this one," Jess says, looking at Saron's phone. "Have you thought a stranger was attractive, but it's fleeting? Like, you think that person is hot, but if you ever pursued it, the feeling would be gone immediately."

"I guess," I say. That's sort of what happened with David. I thought he might be conventionally attractive and that I might like that, but then I kept second-guessing myself, and then I was completely repulsed when we kissed and I felt like I should be into it and I was not into it.

"Do people say you're a prude?" Jess asks.

I think about that night, when I was uncomfortable with Saron walking around in her underwear. I think about all those times I've thought of myself as a prude. "Um," I say. "Maybe."

"Well, you might be demisexual," Saron says. "It's on the gray scale. Under the spectrum of asexuality."

For a second, I think they're making it up, just trying to help me feel better about myself. Except that's ridiculous; they have Google to back them up.

And yet . . . I have heard of asexuality before. There's been a part of my mind that's thought about it, that's thought maybe I'll never feel attraction, but then there would be those glimpses, those brief moments when I was like, *Here we are. I feel it. Here's the proof.*

"Demisexual," I say out loud.

Sammy moves over and sits next to me on the bed. "Yeah, I mean, no pressure. It sounds like that could be it," she says. "But figuring all of this out is a journey, and some people don't like labels, and all of that is okay." She pauses. "I read somewhere that it's like electricity. Some houses always have electricity on. Those are people who aren't on the gray scale. Then there are people who are doing just fine using candles for light—that would be asexuals in this scenario. When you're demi, it's like you use candles until some specific person comes along and turns on the power switch. Does that make sense?" Sammy asks.

Demisexual. And just. I didn't know it was a thing. I didn't know other people felt this way. Demisexual. Demisexual.

This feels . . . big. Like maybe there's an explanation for how I've been feeling.

Then another thought occurs to me: Does this have anything to do with my anxiety? Are they related? Or am I an anxious demisexual? Like a demi with a side helping of panic potatoes. I shake my head. Either way, I need to think more about this. Like, what does this mean for me? Will it change anything? Do I have to tell people about this? It feels like an unnecessary coming out. "Hi, Mom, Dad. I don't like anyone until I get to know them." But that seems kind of like a non-thing. Like duh, don't people want emotional attachments? So how do I explain the rest of it? The fact that I'm repulsed by sexual or romantic contact without those feelings. The worry that there's something deeply wrong with me because I don't act the same way as my friends when it comes to relationships. Is this even something I have to explain to other people?

"You okay?" Saron asks.

Maybe I've been silent too long. Maybe I should be reacting differently. Hugging them? Looking at them, at least, instead of staring, eyes unfocused, at the nightstand between my bed and Saron's?

"Yeah. I mean. Yeah, I'm good. Sorry, it was just. Um . . . Max," I say, picking up my phone from the nightstand. I pretend to look at a message. "Wants to know if I have extra toothpaste, since I'm a better packer."

I don't know why I just lied. I could just say, "Sorry, I don't know how I feel about this demi thing, and I need to process it."

"Boys." Saron rolls her eyes. "Lost without us."

And just like that, I have my out. I grab my key card and my travel toothpaste prop and leave the room.

I can't go to Max, of course. I can't talk to anyone.

I head to the lobby. There's a seating area there with couches that I assume will be empty at this time of night. It looks a little eerie, without the bustle I usually see as we're all walking in or out of the hotel. I find a red leather couch and sit down, my back angled between the seat back and the arm. I pull up my legs, feet resting on the cushion.

Demisexual. I look it up, trying to make sense of it.

There are more articles than I expected to find. I read about the difference between romantic attraction and sexual attraction. I take an online quiz. I read definitions.

And the more I read, the more I feel like it fits. It's a lot, but in a way it's a relief. I'm not broken for feeling repulsed by physical contact. I'm weird in a lot of ways, sure, but not for the way I reacted to David's kiss.

There are other people who feel this way.

I am not alone.

SEASONS OF LOVE

It's Western Wall Day. The holiest of holies, the big spiritual pilgrimage my mom won't stop pestering me about.

I think about Max, still angry with me. I think about Cat. Yeah, I could use some spirituality right now.

All the girls were told that we have to dress respectfully this morning. Just the girls. Dressing respectfully apparently means that we need to have our shoulders covered and skirts/dresses/pants that reach past our knees.

That made Saron huffy. In an act of rebellion, she walked down to the bus in a tube top. She had a jean jacket over it. When Jess gave her a disapproving look, she tugged at her jacket and said, "It buttons up." Then, just for me, she added, "It's one thing to make a choice to dress modestly; it's another to be told you have to."

The old city looks like we stepped straight onto an elaborate movie set, perhaps for some big-budget biblical live-action film starring an inaccurately white cast. That, or we're in the middle of some giant archeological dig, which, to be honest, might be closer to the truth.

There are different sections of the city, divided along religious lines. Chaya explains that we're in the Jewish quarter.

"Jerusalem is one of the key issues that divides Israelis and Palestinians. An obstacle for peace," she says. "I am from Israel; so is my family. No matter what, I speak with that bias. But I want to offer a little bit of the history.

"Obviously, there's a lot of anger and hatred. There is blame on each side. Jews came from all over the world to what is now Israel. They escaped places like Ukraine, Russia, North Africa, many others, where there was antisemitism. Things started earlier with massacres in Eastern Europe and Russia, but a big push to establish Israel was the Holocaust. Some people believed they had a right to return; for others it was about safety." She goes on to mention the British Mandate. "They made promises to Jews and Arabs, promises they did not keep.

"There are two sides to the story. It's complicated. It's complicated because of the history. It's complicated because of the wars. It is complicated because of violence and the different views and opinions on peace."

I think about the current-events class I took, about what Mom has told me. It feels different hearing about this in Jerusalem, the city laid out right in front of me, listening to someone talk about the ground we are standing on, from their perspective. I know I won't ever fully understand what it's like to be on either side of this conflict. But I know I can listen and learn.

Chaya talks more, expanding on the historical importance of Jerusalem to the Jewish people. She tells us a little bit about the Western Wall and the Temple Mount. She reminds us how deeply ingrained the city is in Judaism, noting the phrase spoken at Passover, "Next year in Jerusalem," which is often seen these days as a metaphor for holding on to hope for a better future among a diaspora community.

We continue walking through the old city. Touristy chachkas, or knickknacks, line the streets, from Star of David magnets to mezuzahs and menorahs.

Chaya stops us again, this time at an overlook. My first thought is, *Okay, we are really freaking high up right now; who designed this twisty-turny hill of a city?* I notice the crowds below us, around what looks like just another wall; a wall with a following, sure, but no gold or religious imagery or guardian unicorns in sight. In fact, portions of the Wall have greenery peeking out of them, like the whole thing is overgrown. There are umbrellas connecting to the Wall, like the kind on picnic tables, running down the middle, off-center, forming an exaggerated, misshapen "I." Are there picnic tables in front of the Western Wall?

Sammy leans over. "This is my fourth time here, and I'm still pissed about the two sections." She looks back at the Wall.

I've heard my mom talk about this place a million times. I could teach a class on the history of the temple the Wall belonged to and the cultural significance of the spot. I know how people believe that the prayers they write and place in the cracks of the structure are like pieces of their souls that go directly to G-d. So why don't I know what Sammy is talking about?

"Like, it might be fine if the women's section was the same size," she continues, "but look at the disparity."

That's when I realize that the line down the middle is there to divide men and women. The men's side is almost twice as big as the women's side.

"What?" I ask, pissed. "Why would they do that?"

Sammy shrugs. "Sexism. Also because of Orthodox views, but, like, mostly sexism."

Chaya announces that we have some time to go grab a coffee before we walk down to the Wall. Which would normally make me happy, except I can't stop thinking about the dividing line, splitting the Wall unevenly in two.

Which is definitely my mom's fault for not warning me.

I order an iced coffee, which in Israel is more like a Frappuccino. After I pay, I ask, "Sorry to bother you, but do you have a Wi-Fi password?"

The girl behind the counter nods. She points to a piece of paper taped onto the counter.

I connect to the Wi-Fi and walk to the other side of the store, away from the register. The place is small, but there's enough room so I don't get in the way of the line, which is mostly made up of other people from my group trying to get something to drink during our short break. I take out my earphones and call my mom.

The last time I talked to her was when she brought up therapy. I don't think she'll bring it up again unless I initiate it. I'm not ready to initiate it.

She must have just woken up; I didn't really consider the time difference. She's sitting up in her bed, still wearing a pair of red flannel pajamas. She puts a finger to her lips, then nods to her side. Dad must still be asleep. I watch as she gets out of bed. She walks into my bedroom, just down the hall, and closes the door. "Morning, baby," she says, capped off with a yawn.

"Why didn't you tell me about the Western Wall?" I ask in lieu of a greeting.

"I believe I told you many things about the Wall," she says. She sits down on my bed.

I shake my head. "Not the big gender nonsense stuff," I say. "Why didn't you tell me any of that? It's not fair," I say, feeling childish as the words come out. "You told me I would feel spiritual here, but I don't. I feel angry."

"There's a Yiddish folktale," she starts.

I groan. "This feels like you're avoiding my question."

She shushes me. "Tally, let me finish." She clears her throat. "There's a Yiddish folktale," she starts again, "about a town where all the people are happy. They have everything they could possibly need . . . except salt, so all their food is bland. They come up with a solution: crying. The tears bring flavor to their meals. The bigger meaning is that sadness and grief bring flavor to life."

I crinkle my eyebrows. "Which has to do with the Wall how . . . ?"

"Part of the experience is feeling that anger. The Western Wall is a holy place, a beautiful place with so much history there. But there's also pain and the need for progress.

"In the folktale, the idea was that the Jewish people have experienced hardships, but they don't detract. They add. Grief, sadness, anger, the hardships inform our experiences, but they don't overtake them. You can feel more than one thing at the same time, and those feelings don't invalidate each other." She pauses. Then she adds, "There's a gender-neutral section. It's outside the secured area, but you can still go and visit. Ask your tour leader about it."

I nod.

"Give it a chance," she adds. "Love you, baby."

"Love you," I say back. I stand off to the side for a few moments.

"The hardships inform our experiences." I've been trying for a long time to just ignore anything that feels even a little bit hard. If I pushed it away, I thought I would feel better.

It didn't help, of course.

Cat is still gone. Max is still grieving. Even though it seems like he's processing things much better than I am, he applied to all those schools that are far away. He's going to leave, and I'll be alone.

I had too many feelings, and it was best to just isolate the ones I didn't want to deal with. I'm not sure I'm capable of feeling them all at once.

Maybe I do just need someone to talk to about every-thing. Like a professional who could sort out all my messes and teach me techniques to process my emotions and— Oh, right.

That's called therapy.

After the coffee break, we walk down to the Wall. We go in through the security as a group. Just after Chaya releases us, I ask about the other section. "Hey, um, I heard there's a gender-neutral area," I try.

Chaya smiles. "Yes, would you like to see?"

A few other people join us. We walk out the side exit, past security, until we reach an area that looks like we're in the middle of some archeological dig. There are stones poking out of the earth, unorganized rubble beneath a walkway, raised above the mass of stones.

It's small, even smaller than the women-only section. But.

I think about all the feelings I tried to suppress: Cat's death, Max leaving, even all my confusion around David and our kiss. The feelings start to build on one another, jumbled together. There's more, too, like going to Yad Vashem and finding out where our relatives were murdered during the Holocaust and still not feeling Jewish enough. Good things start to work their way in too: I picture Saron drawing and Joshua and Gabriel taking pictures with the banner and David giving me a high five after we found the *Ahava* statue.

All these feelings make me think about where I'm standing, this ancestral connection that I wasn't really expecting I would feel.

I start to cry. I'm not sure why I feel this way now when the other area, the area I was supposed to feel a connection to, just made me really angry. I guess it's those roots; I guess I'm finally feeling that spiritual connection Mom kept talking about.

Chaya puts her arm on my shoulder. "I know," she says. She lets go, walks over to the railing, pulls out a neatly folded sheet of paper and a pen from her purse, and starts writing.

I'm supposed to write a prayer now.

When you write a prayer for the Western Wall, it's said to be a part of your soul. The letters are even collected, twice a year, and given a proper Jewish burial.

The only paper I have is in my musical notebook. I rip out a page and I write. I write my prayer as a letter.

Dear G-d,

    I think I've been angry with you for a while. For a lot of reasons . . . For Cat's death and hurting Max and my loneliness and confusion and a million other things. For giving me more than I can handle by myself.

    I don't understand why you took her. I don't understand what the point was in that. I don't understand how a higher power can even exist with half the mess going on in the world.

    I haven't understood a lot of things lately.

    I want to believe that there are reasons. I want to believe that even though I am hurting, I can heal. I want to believe.

    I bet Cat is causing all kinds of trouble in whatever spiritual afterworld you have cooked up. Look out for her in ways I couldn't.

    Love,
    Tally

I fold it up, small enough to fit in a crack in the Wall. I don't feel right taking a picture of myself in front of the Wall—it seems too touristy, too superficial—but I do take a picture of my letter.

We regroup and head back to the bus so we can go to Ben Yehuda Street for lunch. Once we're seated and journeying to food, I take a look at my picture.

There's my prayer sticking out of a crack in the Wall. There's one word visible on the folded piece of paper.

Love,

Love. Comma.

Love to something higher, something beyond my understanding. Love plus, punctuation that guarantees more.

I'm thinking about Cat again. I'm thinking about how I can love her and more. I can love her and hate her. I can miss her. I can remember her. I can mourn.

It's like you can't mourn. I hear Max's voice in my head. Max. Has he been feeling like this the whole time? I saw everything he was doing as a cry for help, a need to be fixed, but he's been doing better than I have all along.

He got help, real help that I'm still too scared to ask for; he let himself feel his mess of emotions, and I don't even know how to function with them all swirling around my mind without crying.

I think I owe him an apology. I think, at the very least, we need to talk.

I look over. He's sitting near the back of the bus with Joshua and Gabriel, talking animatedly and using his hands for emphasis.

I just hope he'll be able to forgive me.

I take out my music notebook and start a new song. I might not be able to process everything now, but maybe this will help.

YOU MATTER TO ME

"Flower crowns," Joshua says. "For each of us."

We're standing in the shuk after lunch as Joshua plans for the perfect Pride experience.

"Do you think they sell face paint here too?" he continues. "You know what, I bet you someone at the parade will have some. Worse comes to worst, we'll use that eye shadow palette Saron brought with her. It has all the colors of the rainbow, right?"

"Yes, because girls often paint rainbows on their faces. With eye shadow," she deadpans. "I splurged and got the special kind that comes with unicorn tattoos."

"Are they sparkly?" he asks, voice serious.

Saron closes her eyes like she's searching for peace in a chaotic world.

"No matter what, we need the flower crowns," he continues. "Need."

Joshua must have some kind of magic in his blood because he finds the flower crowns at the first touristy store we visit. "I look best in pink, so this one is mine," he says, trying on a headband adorned with fake pale-pink flowers. "I look good, right? Of course I look good; I'm wearing a flower crown. Okay, everyone else needs to pick out their flowers!"

We comply like the good, supportive friends we clearly are.

I do a little more shopping and round up some gifts. A key chain, a postcard.

I spot a notebook, propped up on the counter. I've been thinking about getting a new one, and this is so pretty, a pale-blue leather embossed with a pattern of navy Stars of David. I hold it in my hands, feeling the indents of the stars. I flip through the pages, looking at the lined space and off-white paper. I wonder what songs I could write on these pages.

We make our purchases with enough time to wander through the shuk before it's time for Jerusalem Pride.

I'm going. I'm definitely going. I mean, who would pass up an opportunity like this? I have to go.

I think about the articles I read last night and the confusion I felt around touch and attraction for a long time. I think about the difference between kissing David and giving him a high five. Does this mean Pride applies to me? I'm just starting to figure it all out, but it feels deeply important to go to the parade.

The danger thing, that's still real. But I'm safe with our

group, I remind myself. I'm totally safe. I'm going to be totally safe.

We get off the bus a few blocks away from an entrance point. Most everyone is going, with a few stragglers staying behind on the bus. David is chaperoning the bus folks.

Chaya leads the way with Jess. Batya takes up the rear.

There's not a lot of room on the sidewalk. I end up walking in step with Gabriel.

We're quiet for a while before he asks, "Have you ever been to Pride before?"

I shake my head. "Not a huge fan of crowds. Plus, I'm not sure it's my place."

"Straight?" he asks.

"Um." I'm not sure how I'm supposed to respond. Do I explain the demi thing? Is this what I am now? Does this change who I am?

"Actually, I'm demisexual," I test the words. "I think? I'm still figuring it out."

"Ace spectrum, cool."

"Yeah," I say. "But, like. I just don't know if that means I can be a part of Pride."

"I don't think there's any intruding, since the point is really about acceptance. Loving and expressing that love in your own way," he says.

"Is it unfair of me to lump myself in with people who have it harder?" I ask. "Like, I might end up happily with some boy and fit into heteronormative standards."

"I might end up with a girl. Doesn't make me less bi.

Doesn't mean I still don't find dudes sexy. But I get it; I've worried about that stuff too."

I nod. We keep walking, quietly now, a few paces behind the rest of our group.

After much maneuvering, Chaya finds us an entrance that isn't jam-packed.

Once we are all gathered in the line, Jess walks up to the front of the group. "Everyone. Eyes up here. Don't make me clap to get your attention." She pauses and waits for us. "All right, there are a lot of people here. So we're going to do a buddy system. You *must* always be with your buddy. Go get a buddy."

Saron grabs my hand before I can even look around. "You're mine," she says.

"You don't go *anywhere* without your buddy. Or an adult. Stay with the adults."

"We're all very mature," Joshua says.

Jess ignores him. "Stay with the staff members," she continues, voice unwaveringly firm. "I'm serious—you're all going to be ridiculously safe or else."

"They're fine," Chaya says.

Jess doesn't seem so sure.

We go through security and get Pride wristbands before we find a space to sit. The marching part of the parade won't start for at least another half hour. We're sitting on a patch of grass, waiting for the parade to begin. There are some speakers by a big stage they have set up, but keeping us all together to go and listen to the speeches seems like too much effort.

Chaya almost immediately gets up to go say hello to people, which does not help calm down Jess.

Things get worse when we lose Joshua and Gabriel.

"How can you not know where they went?" Jess asks, staring directly at Saron.

"Excuse me, I'm not their keeper. Plus, I'm not the one who lost a buddy. My buddy is right here." She points to me. "I'm clearly innocent in all this."

"You were supposed to be more responsible; you know I can't trust them to take care of themselves. If they wind up dead, I swear you'll all be joining—"

"Guys," Joshua interrupts, walking back over. "I found the face paint."

"Where's your buddy?" Jess asks, exasperated.

"I left him getting his face painted. There's face paint. Why is no one listening to me about this? Come on." He is already walking back through the crowd.

"All right, whoever is interested, grab your buddies. Everyone else, stay here with Batya." Jess stands up. "I guess we're getting our faces painted."

We manage to keep track of Joshua bopping through the crowd. He stops at a kids' playground.

The swing set has been converted into a makeup station. Gabriel is sitting on a swing, getting a rainbow butterfly painted onto one of his cheeks. He has a bi flag on the other.

"Bro, you look hot," Joshua says. I swear, Gabriel's cheeks get a little red at that, and not just because of the paint.

"You are a friend of Chaya too?" the man who is running this playground makeup station asks.

"Chaya?" Jess asks.

"Well, yeah, who do you think showed us this place?" Joshua asks, as though it were obvious all along.

"Fine, okay. Where did she go, then?"

The man nods to the stage.

Chaya is standing at the podium with a group of teenagers around her. I think they're crying.

"Why does she have to be like this when I'm frustrated?" Jess doesn't really look frustrated right now. She's looking a little bit more like the heart-eyes emoji.

"Who's next?" the man asks.

We take turns getting a little splash of rainbow on our faces. Joshua manages to find a rainbow makeup stick, which I didn't even know existed, and draws a rainbow mustache and goatee on by himself.

"Anyone else want to come to Boutique Josh-u-amazing?"

Saron rolls her eyes. "We're sticking with the professional, thanks."

When it's my turn, I sit down on the swing and it sways a little. This is weird. I shouldn't be here. I don't know this person; who the hell just paints random people's faces?

I take a breath. I'm safe.

"You want a rainbow? A flag? Bi flag? You are bi? Lesbian?"

I try it out again. "I'm demisexual . . . I think. It's new."

"Ah, gray, yes. I can do gray."

Mr. Paint goes to work, and I try my best not to wobble on the swing. Gray? Is he just going to smear my face in gray now?

247

I wonder if that's to stand for sexuality or lack thereof. Like if my sexuality is muted, everything else should be muted too.

"Okay, done now. Very simple, yeah." The man has a handheld mirror, one of those old-fashioned ones that are used in kids' art classes to do self-portraits. He painted another butterfly for me, this time outlined in gray. The inside has white, gray, black, and purple stripes.

It doesn't look muted. It looks beautiful, crisp and clear with a pop of bright purple.

"You're missing something," Saron says. She finds the rainbow stick Joshua put back with the other supplies. "Stay still—this is really going to bring it all together. Okay, done!" She backs away.

"I look ridiculous, don't I?" I ask.

"Not in the slightest," Saron assures.

"She drew a Dali mustache on you; didn't you feel it?" Joshua jokes, standing by her side.

Saron gives him a quick glare. "Here, give me a hot sec." She snaps a picture of me and then practically shoves her phone in my face. "See, adorable."

My curls are a little messy hanging down around my shoulders, my typical ponytail sacrificed to show off the purple flower crown atop my head, and I have an asexual spectrum butterfly on one cheek and a rainbow streak on the other, but I do actually look pretty adorable. I smile.

"Told ya," Saron says proudly.

I look good. I look good in rainbow and gray scale and adorned with a flower crown.

I feel good too. Or rather, I feel a lot of things all at once, because the anxiety is still there and missing Cat is still there but that doesn't dull my other feelings.

The tears bring flavor. I don't have to pretend that the tears aren't there anymore.

I see Max sitting alone on the bridge between the slide and a rope ladder, his feet dangling off the side.

I join him.

"Hi, Moxie," I start softly.

He doesn't respond.

I consider telling him about Mom's folktale or trying to explain how scared I've been to let myself feel anything real. I think about how I have been using him as a distraction so I wouldn't have to think about myself. I don't know how to say any of that in a way that would make sense.

Instead, I say, "You don't need to be fixed. I'm sorry for . . . well, for everything."

He looks over at me. "I think I should probably be sorry too."

I snort. "Right. Because you were the one trying to squash out all signs of grief."

"I'm not saying you were right," he points out. "Because you weren't. You did a lot of bad things. Made many terrible decisions. Really unhealthy, terrible decisions."

"This is helping," I say sarcastically.

"But," he continues, "I should have seen what was going on. I should have known you were hurting too. I shouldn't have told anyone before you were ready to talk. Tal, are you okay?" he asks.

I shrug. "I don't think I've been okay for a while." I swing my legs a little, now dangling from the side of the bridge.

"It's okay not to be okay."

I nod.

It hasn't felt that way, though. I was convinced I needed to take control, to grab on to what little I had left of my future. Max was the one who was still here, so his part of the plan was what I could save.

If he was still here, I wouldn't be alone.

"I think I was just scared about losing you too," I say. "I mean, we had all these plans, and then Cat died and everything just fell apart. I thought maybe I could salvage some of it if we still went to school together. I don't know. That's silly."

"Totally ridiculous," he agrees.

I hit his arm.

"No, I get it," he says. "I just couldn't see that future anymore. It didn't seem possible, so I had to find another way." He pauses. "You know, even if we aren't in school together next year, I'll still be there for you."

He puts his arm around my shoulder, squeezes, and then lets go.

"I'll be there for you too," I say. "For real this time."

He looks at my makeup. "Is this new?" he asks, pointing to the butterfly.

"I guess," I say. "I think maybe it has been this way for a while, but I didn't know other people felt the same way. That there was a name for it."

He nods. "Makes sense."

"I just wish I could talk to Cat about it. She was the first person I wanted to tell," I continue. "There are so many things I wish I could tell her."

"Sometimes I still talk to her," Max says. "I even sent her a text message once. I wonder if her mom read it."

We're quiet, looking out over the crowds.

"Do you remember that time Mom and Dad rented that house on the Cape and Cat lived with us for six weeks?" Max asks. "She was such a jerk that summer. She kept locking me outside."

I can picture it perfectly, see Max at thirteen with his face pressed up against the glass door of the house. I can even hear him pounding his fists against the door, yelling that it really wasn't funny anymore. "Remember that one time it rained and Mom and Dad were at the grocery store and Cat just sat there and watched you get drenched through the window?"

"Do you remember when she left me those creepy threatening notes inside my video game cases?"

"I might have helped with those," I admit. "But the undershirts, that was all her."

"I can't believe she went and bought tie-dye for that." He shakes his head. "She was the worst. I miss her so much."

"I know." I roll my right ankle, keeping my eyes on my feet, the ground below us slightly out of focus.

"It helps me to remember," he says.

"I think it might help me too."

Saron walks over and stops near the bottom of the slide. "Move your tuchuses—the march is starting!"

We leave the playground and we march. We march as a group; we march as people who are gay and lesbian and bisexual and ace spectrum and straight and don't like labels. And it's not scary, not like I thought it would be. I feel strong.

As we walk out of the park, most of us are handed flowers. I'm not sure why until we get about two blocks away.

It's for a memorial. The girl who died. We take turns placing the flowers by her picture.

I put my flower down for this girl. I think of another girl too, the one who I loved and lost.

I'm overcome with this feeling of honor. This feeling of respect and love. The memorial, the flowers, the man who painted our faces, the speeches, the flags, the signs.

And in this space that should make me feel all sorts of terrified, I feel completely safe and inspired.

YOU WILL BE FOUND

We pack up after dinner. It's Saron's idea. She thinks it's the responsible thing to do, since we need to be ready for our full day of flying tomorrow. "Plus, I don't want it to worry any of us when we spend the whole night partying it up."

As I'm sorting through my stuff, I find Saron's necklace. The one she made me wear on our very first day in Israel.

I walk over to her, packing on the other side of the room. "I thought it might be time to return this," I say.

"Memories, huh," she says, taking the necklace.

"That first day when you told me what to wear . . . Who knew we'd become so close?"

"I knew," Saron says. "I knew all along, Tally Mark."

We finish gathering our things. Our room, now lined with packed suitcases, is the meeting point for the group.

"I have a game," Saron offers, holding up one of the now-empty bottles of wine. We're all settled in our room now, spread out across the beds or sitting on the floor.

"Spin the Bottle?" Sammy asks.

"Of course not. But kind of." Saron shrugs. "Think more sharing and less making out. The rules are simple," she continues. "The bottle lands on you, you share a memory from the trip."

"How mushy," Jess says. "I love it."

Saron holds up the bottle, pointing the top to herself. "For example, remember when we went rafting and the ridiculous thing barely moved?"

"I thought we were going to be stuck in the Jordan River forever," Sammy says with an exaggerated sigh.

What do I remember from rafting? I think I was obsessing over whether Max was interacting with everyone else . . . particularly Sammy. Did I ruin my own trip trying to distract myself from how I was really feeling?

Saron spins the bottle, and it lands on Joshua.

"Remember when I found the flower crowns and the face painting?" he asks.

"That was literally earlier today," Gabriel says.

"I know; wasn't it great?" Joshua smiles. He's still wearing his flower crown.

He spins the bottle, and it lands on Max. "I loved our New Year's Eve celebration," he says.

I wasn't even there at the celebration because I was talking to David.

I liked talking to David that night. I liked the intimacy of sitting alone, at night, in the middle of the desert, talking until the New Year.

Do I like David romantically? I'm not sure. I'm still trying to figure out my sexuality, and I'm not sure this is the right time to be thinking about anyone in particular. Especially since this trip is ending.

The bottle lands on Jess. "Hmm." She taps her chin. "Last night was pretty great, the parts I remember, at least." She winks at Saron. "Oh, I don't know; I loved so much of it! Hiking and seeing the Western Wall and meeting the Israelis. Meeting all of you!" She sighs. "I can't believe this is our last night."

This *is* our last night, and I'm only now realizing that I wasted this trip. Why am I incapable of appreciating the things around me? I spent too much time being anxious and fighting. I should've stayed in the moment; I should've focused on the activities and the people and the places and—

I'm on the verge of a spiral when the bottle lands on me. I swallow hard. What do I say?

I didn't expect most of this trip. I hoped I would see Uncle Ezzie; I knew I would see places in Israel, the country where Safta grew up. But I didn't know I would see the actual place where she used to live. I didn't think I'd find out about demisexuality. I knew I wanted time with Max, but I didn't think we would protect each other and fight and talk about Cat. I didn't think we would become this close with anyone else on the trip.

I think about talking to Max on the playground and marching with the whole group. I felt so . . . present. I don't want to let go of that feeling.

"All right," I say at last. "Pride meant a lot to me today."

Saron raises her glass. "What a great choice."

The thing is, it feels like the *right* choice. No worries, no pressure. I can be here right now with everyone, living in this moment.

We play a few more rounds, but it somehow devolves into Saron ranting about Hallmark Christmas movies as Joshua paces the room trying to come up with a solution for his banner problem and the group naturally divides into smaller conversations.

Which is how I end up chatting with Sammy.

I'm not sure what to say to her at first. We've been spending time together but mostly in groups. Part of the problem is that I feel guilty. I was essentially using her, trying to turn her into a solution to stop Max from grieving. I didn't stop to think about her as a person, beyond her mention of thinking my brother was cute. I don't even know if she would want to be set up. I know I wouldn't. Maybe she has anxiety; maybe she's on the ace spectrum. I have no idea.

When I did think of her as an individual, I was jealous. She was more visibly Jewish in her day-to-day life, which made me feel lesser.

There's no legitimate reason for me to feel this way. She has been nothing but kind. I remember earlier today when she told me about her frustrations with the Western Wall. She could have brought this up with the larger group, but she confided in me.

Which is why I tell her the story about the tears.

". . . and that's why my mom didn't warn me," I say. "She had cooked this up as a teachable moment."

Sammy shakes her head in disbelief, like this is the coolest story she's ever heard. "Can I tell you something?" she asks, her voice sounding nervous. "I'm a little jealous," she says.

"What?" I ask, taken aback.

"Growing up like that, learning about all the history, it's nothing like how I was raised," she explains. "In my family, we were taught to believe everything at temple, no digging deeper. I never really felt connected to my faith until I started doing my own research." She pauses. "I really want to study religion in college, but I'm not sure my parents would support it," she says in a rush. "I never actually said that out loud before." She puts a hand over her mouth like she can't believe she just let it out.

"Have you applied to BU?" I ask. "My mom's a pretty great teacher."

"I haven't, actually," she says.

"Well," I say, "the deadline is in two days. You still have time."

She smiles. "I think I'll give it a shot."

I imagine her applying and getting in. I imagine us sharing a room on campus. I imagine us still having time to learn more about each other.

Joshua audibly gasps from across the room.

"I figured it out!"

The different conversations quiet down, our attention now turned to Joshua.

"The fashion show didn't work because it just featured

the two of us." He waves toward Gabriel. "That's not the spirit of the banner. Sure, it started as a joke between Gabriel and me, but it's more now. Tattoos wouldn't have realistically worked because, again, it would have been just us."

"I'm not sure I agreed to get a tattoo," Gabriel interjects. "I was only being supportive."

That doesn't stop Joshua. "What we need, what we've needed all along, is something for everyone. Boxers out!"

He sends us all to collect our Israeli flag boxers and scavenges for some permanent markers.

"I have some!" Jess says cheerfully. "I bought a multicolored pack for the poster I made when you guys arrived at the airport." She leaves the room, then comes back with a pack of twelve permanent markers.

"We should invite David," I say.

Saron raises an eyebrow. "Oh, should we?"

"He's sort of been a part of the group," I say, blushing.

"I can text him," Jess says, already typing on her phone.

Five minutes later, he arrives at the door holding the boxers Joshua gave him last night. "What exactly is going on here?" he asks.

Joshua's plan has two parts. First, he has all of us pass around the boxers, our names written on the laundry-instruction tags. He writes #IVEGOTCHUTZPAH on all the waistbands. Then we each sign, writing little notes to one another like these are pages in a yearbook.

The second part of his plan is a group picture.

Jess volunteers to take the photo.

"All right, everyone! Smile!" she directs.

We're all standing together, wearing our signed boxers over our clothes like a silly uniform, with Joshua and Gabriel holding out the banner in front of us.

"This is perfect!" Joshua declares, eyeing the group. "All right, photographer, send it to everyone!"

"We need a group chat," Sammy points out.

Which is how we all end up in a group chat called the Jew Crew, a way for all of us to keep in touch after we get back from the trip.

It really is what the banner would have wanted.

GOODBYE UNTIL TOMORROW/ I COULD NEVER RESCUE YOU

In the morning, we bring our bags down to the lobby and start saying our goodbyes. Most of us are heading to the airport, but Jess is staying in Jerusalem with Chaya for a full month.

I realize that I'll miss them.

The rest of us head to the airport. We leave our bags at the baggage check and go through security. We find our gate. We board the airplane.

My second time on a plane in less than two weeks. I'm too exhausted to be worried.

I try to get some sleep. I have an eye mask and an airplane-issued blanket, which is currently secured underneath my seat belt. I stayed up too late writing last night. I don't regret it; writing felt like a good way to work through my feelings. Plus, I have the time to sleep now.

Or I would have the time if it weren't for Saron.

"Switch with me," she says, snapping the sleep mask against my face.

I frown and pull up the fabric off one eye. "What?"

"Switch with me. Max clearly does not want to sleep right now, and the losers I was stuck next to are all trying to sleep anyway, so . . ."

I pull the mask back down.

"31D, we're switching," she says. She bends down, undoes my seat belt, and pulls me up from my seat.

I huff, move the mask to the top of my head, and wrap my airplane-issued blanket around my shoulders like a cape.

"Can't you just sleep a little cuter? Maybe tame that hair a little? Add some lip color?"

I tilt my head like a confused puppy. "Sleep cuter?"

"Never mind. 31D, off you go!"

I grumble my way to my new seat and immediately realize the reason Saron wanted to switch.

"David," I say.

"Tally."

I sit down next to him. "Saron told me everyone was sleeping over here, so . . ."

"I could sleep. I wasn't going to, but sleep sounds like the smartest option."

"Self-care," I say. "It's no hats and water bottles, but I guess sleep will do."

We're both quiet for a few seconds, and then I say, "Or we could talk."

"Yes, the smartest-er option," he says. "I was just thinking we needed a proper trip debriefing."

"But that would require a conference room and a horde of Jewish youths," I say in my best taken-aback tone.

"I've heard you can make do with just two of them," he says.

"As long as they're the right two," I add. "And as long as they're on a plane."

"So what's the final verdict on the trip? Do you feel more Jewish now?" he asks.

"I secretly became a rabbi on day two and no one noticed."

"I knew there was something different about you, but I just couldn't put my finger on it," he says. "Did you discover anything?" he continues.

"I did, actually," I say. "You?"

"Many, many things. Like my knack for self-defense and uncanny ability to uncover adventures."

"Is this about Om-lantis again?" I ask.

"It's always about Om-lantis," he says with a smile.

Completely subjectively, it's a very cute smile.

Like his personality is written all over his face.

"David, can I ask you something?" I say.

"That's the point of a debrief, Tally."

"No, but I mean, without joking. I even promise I won't make any cheese-related puns."

"Well, that is serious. Shoot."

"Do you think that this made a difference? Like, will we all keep in touch or hang out? Other than when the Israelis come over for their trip."

"I don't think we'll wear matching boxers at the same time again, that's for sure. Some people will stay in touch but definitely not everyone. But does that mean it didn't make a difference? Nah, I mean, look at you!"

"I'm a rabbi now," I say.

"Yes. Yes, you are."

We're quiet again until I say, "David."

"Tally?"

"I'm happy I got to discover with you."

"Me too."

I smile at him, and for once, I don't feel an ounce of anxiety.

⟹ ———— ⟸

I decide to reclaim my seat about halfway through the flight.

"You were gone for a very long time." Saron waggles her eyebrows. She puts down her sketchbook, balancing it on the seat-back tray.

The seat next to her is available. "Where's Max?" I ask.

She nods in his direction, a few rows over. He's standing in the aisle, talking to Sammy.

I sit down in his seat. "Did you do this?"

"I swear, he walked over there all by himself," she says. "I'm completely innocent."

"Completely? Not in my experience."

"How *was* David?" she asks. "Did you have a good time over there?"

"I slept," I say.

"You joined the mile-high club?"

"Definitely not what I just said," I point out. "We talked, and then I slept. Better?"

"I'll accept it," she decides. "Though the mile-high-club thing was more of what I was shooting for."

"Yes," I say. "Very clever with this whole switching business."

"Oh, no, I was really smart about this whole thing. I didn't just do it with you. I changed my seat so I could be next to Joshua and then got Gabriel to swap with me. Then I did it for, like, three other rando should-be couples. They didn't get enough screen time in this masterpiece I call life, so I thought I'd just leave them the parting gift of true love."

"Matchmaker, matchmaker," I say, shaking my head in bemusement.

"Did you at least have a good talk?" she asks.

I roll my eyes. "We proposed to each other simultaneously."

"If that's the case, I get to be maid of honor, Tally Mark. Because of all the hard work I put into this," she says.

"We exchanged US phone numbers," I admit. "Happy?"

"Very."

I look over at her sketchbook. "That's beautiful," I say.

She smiles. "I figured out the concept for the final piece in my portfolio." She picks up her design so I can have a better look.

There are four different models on the page, each with a dress made of rectangular cutouts, all pieced together, the sharp lines uneven around their necks like columns that start in different places.

"They're letters," she explains. "My goal is to have it look like the Western Wall from far away, but when you get closer, you can see that each one is a prayer. I'm hoping to get different people to write them and then piece them all together. I think this might be it." Her voice is excited. "No matter what happens with the applications, I definitely want to use this idea at some point."

I look closer at her work. I have no doubt that she'll turn the concept into a real project.

I notice something about one of the models. Each one is a different size and height, the lines smoothly curling on the page. The third model sketched on the page looks familiar. The shape of her eyes, the curves of her arms and torso.

"Is that me?" I ask.

She grins, an almost mischievous uptick to her lips. "I made you a model. I'm going to force you to wear it and walk down a runway someday."

"Right," I say, like it will never happen.

But maybe I will be in a Saron-styled fashion show. Maybe I'll keep in touch with her and she'll actually end up being my maid of honor. We live near each other. We have the rest of our senior year to hang out. And after that, who knows.

My future is so unknown. I used to have a perfect plan for everything.

But now . . . now I don't know anything. Which isn't awesome for my anxiety, but it is a little freeing too.

TOMORROW

I'm not sure if I'm still running on Israeli time, but I wake up really early the next day, and I can't go back to sleep. I have a new idea.

I get out of bed, stretching my too-stiff arms, and walk over to my suitcase. All my clothes from the trip definitely need to be washed, I think as I sort through my bag. I find what I'm looking for near the bottom, tucked into a corner with some of the other souvenirs I collected on the trip.

The new journal with Stars of David lining the cover. I grab some other notebooks, a few stacked on my bookcase and one carefully placed in my carry-on bag.

I transcribe the songs I was working on in Israel, all messy in the notebook Cat gave me, neatly into my new Israeli journal. I add some of my other favorite songs from over the years, some of the silly ones I made up for Cat when we were little, and a few from the gathered notebooks that are now scattered on my duvet.

I write one more.

"Goodbye Now"

I can't say goodbye now
You won't get that
I don't like goodbyes now
Because some words, they just fall flat.

So I'll see you again
We'll talk once more soon
A call now and then
I'll write you a tune
You're there in my thoughts
These memories clear
We all get our lots in this life and I miss you, my dear

I need you, goodbye now
I miss you, goodbye now
I love you, goodbye now
You're with me, goodbye now

I don't need goodbyes
Now that I know
It's time to let go
I love you, you know

I love you
I know

I close Cat's notebook and place it on my nightstand, laying the pen by its side. I take the new one, now filled with my favorite songs, written in my neatest handwriting, and clutch it to my chest. I can do this.

I pull on a thick maroon sweater and gray leggings and head to Max's room, knocking three times on his door before opening. He's not there, so I head downstairs.

I find Max sitting at the kitchen table, eating a bowl of cereal.

"Moxie, can I ask you for a favor?"

He looks up, mid-bite.

"Could you go with me to visit Cat? I can't go alone."

He puts down his spoon, balancing it against his cereal bowl. "Of course," he says.

I wait for Max as he changes out of his pajamas, sitting on the living room couch with the notebook on my lap. I flip through the pages a few more times to make sure everything is perfect and then tuck it into my purse.

"Is this . . . appropriate?" Max asks, walking down the stairs. He's wearing jeans and a striped blue button-down.

"I don't think there's a dress code," I say, tugging at my sweater. Is there a dress code? Should I change? Are you supposed to wear black to a cemetery? Is there some sort of etiquette I don't know about?

It's winter; we're putting on puffy coats, I remind myself. Even if there is a secret dress code, we'll be fine.

The air is so cold that I'm ready to empty my savings account and book a flight back to Israel. I get in the passenger's seat of Mom's car, reaching in the back to grab the BU blanket she keeps folded under the seat during the winter. Max can't fight me on this; it's my school.

Maybe it will be his too. Maybe not.

He turns on the car, the glass fogging from the new heat, and we head to the cemetery.

The last time I went to the cemetery was for the burial. There wasn't a headstone. They take a while to make, apparently. There is one now; I can see it ahead of us. I stop and look at the other graves. I'm not sure what I believe about the afterlife, but there's a part of me that feels like she knows we're here.

We walk up closer.

I touch the strap of my purse, absentmindedly pulling it closer.

I can't do this. We should leave now. I need to leave now; I need to—

No. No, I don't need to go. I need to be right here.

But that doesn't mean I have to go first.

"You start," I say.

Max talks for a while. He tells Cat about the trip, about the schools he applied to for next fall. I think maybe he forgot that I'm standing there, too, until he says, "Your turn."

Should I say something to her? Can I?

What would I even say out loud? I don't know how to verbalize missing her. All my emotions still feel so mixed, so unmanageable. Should I talk to her like I would if she were still alive? Tell her about the trip? Tell her about David?

I want to, I really do, but how the hell am I supposed to deal with the fact that she won't respond?

I take a small step forward. I have to say something. "Um, hi," I start.

I don't know what else to say. I grip the notebook, like maybe some of the words inside will help me talk.

"I was stuck," I finally get out, eyes on the light-blue cover. "Even before . . . even before you were gone, I was so stuck. I was worried about applying to schools and how I look and just . . . It got worse without you. Everything got worse.

"I wrote these for you," I continue. "And I'm going to keep trying to write. I'm not . . . I'm not always good with talking. I keep so much in my head, and then I'm convinced I'll just say it all wrong. But with these"—I hold up the songs—"I can say it all."

I take another step closer. "It's a Jewish custom to place rocks on a headstone as a sign of respect and to show you were there and, um." I pause. "I know you're not Jewish, but I thought I'd leave this here." I place the notebook on top of her headstone.

I look back at Max. He's taken a few steps away to give me some privacy. "I was thinking about Mount Herzl," I say to him. "There was that one grave with all those tokens around it. Not just the rocks. The lanyards and hats and water bottles and pictures. And, well, I owed her some songs."

"She would have loved them," he says.

"I know."

Mom is awake when we get home.

"You kids left early," she notes. She's standing by the kitchen counter, fixing herself a cup of coffee.

"Still on Israeli time," I say.

She pours milk in her cup. "Want anything for break-fast?" she asks.

"Already ate," Max answers. "I have plans. Some of the guys were thinking about getting the old band together," he explains. "Want to come?"

I shake my head. I have something else I need to do. "Have fun," I say. "Maybe I'll come to your first concert."

He laughs. "We're messing around in a garage," he says.

"Can't wait for the big stadium show."

He rolls his eyes. "Weirdo." He says his goodbyes by hugging Mom and then walking over to me and ruffling my hair like I'm a child.

I go to the counter next to Mom, smoothing my hair. I pick up Mom's mug and take a sip.

"Could you pretty please . . . ?" I start.

She sighs. "I'll make another one. You kids are too much; I'm sending you back to Israel."

I smile, still holding the cup of coffee she just made. I can do this.

I think about all those feelings that have been jumbled up in my head, how anxious I was on the trip.

I remind myself how good it felt to talk to Max before the Pride parade. *It's okay not to be okay.*

It's okay to ask for help too, I tell myself.

I clear my throat. I'm just going to say it. Now. No, now. No— "I'm ready to go to therapy," I say.

I'm not sure what I expected Mom's reaction would be. Cheers? Confetti? A disappointed and concerned look? A lecture on how she knew all along this was what I needed?

She doesn't even look up from the new cup of coffee she's pouring.

"Sounds good," Mom says simply, like it isn't a big deal. I had built it up in my head as the biggest of big deals, but all Mom has to do is call and make an appointment, which she does after we finish eating breakfast. It's so completely easy; I don't know why I was worried. I don't know why I stress about half the things that run through my head.

I guess I can talk about that with Dr. Rosen next Thursday.

I go back upstairs to my room after breakfast and take Cat's musical notebook off my nightstand. I run my fingers along the indents on the cover, the musical notes to some unknown song.

I open it up to a blank page.

I take the pen I used earlier off my nightstand. From the corner of my eye, I see my phone light up with a text from David.

I smile. I'll respond to him after I write.

And I'm not sure what this new song is going to be about yet, but I start planning.

I'll figure it out along the way.

A NOTE FROM THE AUTHOR

I began writing the first draft of *Once More with Chutzpah* shortly after my first trip to Israel. I will forever be grateful that I had the chance to attend Jerusalem Pride, visit the gender-neutral section of the Western Wall, and see my Safta's homeland. I even got the chance to meet her cousins, who grew up with her like siblings, for the first time.

This book is a work of fiction. I took several liberties, ranging from the specifics of the temple high school exchange program to moving Jerusalem Pride to January (it was in August when I went) so the characters could attend. I also realized it was important to acknowledge certain cultural elements that some readers may not be aware of, like the fact that there are no standard translations for Hebrew words into English. The most common example many people are familiar with is Chanukah/Hanukkah, though my particular favorite is Safta/Savta.

I included many details from my own trip, but some didn't fit precisely into Tally's story. I was older than Tally when I visited, and I remember sitting in on a professor's academic lecture on the Middle Eastern conflict and stopping outside a checkpoint. While those experiences aren't echoed exactly in *Once More with Chutzpah*, it was important for me to give my characters other opportunities to explore some of the perspectives I encountered. These moments were and are immensely meaningful to me, both as a Jewish American and someone with Israeli family facing the country's history and living in its complex present. Throughout this entire writing and publication journey, it's been important to me to listen, learn, and think critically about the nuanced aspects of my own cultural background.

That said, this is, ultimately, one story. The complete story of the Middle East includes many other voices, including those of young people who live in Palestine or are of Palestinian descent. I also hope to read more stories from across the diaspora about Jewish identity and anxiety and asexuality, and I feel so unbelievably lucky to have made this contribution.

Thank you for reading Tally's story!

—Haley

ACKNOWLEDGMENTS

This is my first time writing out acknowledgments. As a person with anxiety, I am very deeply convinced that I will miss someone. So sorry, guys. In advance. Just in case.

My name is on the cover, but there are so many incredibly talented people who put in the work to make sure that this book would even exist in the first place. Thank you a million times over to Team Triada, especially my agent, Lauren Spieller, who helped me rip apart this story and turn it into a novel. I am humbled to have you in my corner.

To my Bloomsbury team, wow. You all are almost too good? Thank you to my editor, Allison Moore, for her perfect notes. Your vision made OMWC possible. Someday I hope I get to take you to a Broadway show so we can fangirl together. Thank you to Erica Barmash, Faye Bi, Beth Eller, Jasmine Miranda, Diane Aronson, Donna Mark, Anahzsa Jones, and everyone else at Bloomsbury who worked on this book. And thank you to Leni Kauffman and Jeanette Levy for the beautiful cover.

My writing family, thank you forever and always. Thank you to Courtney Escoyne, who read every single draft of this book, even the bad ones (or, rather, *especially* the bad ones). You are my writing person through and through. Saying this book wouldn't exist without you feels too small. To Auriane Desombre, for teaching me everything I know about publishing, and to her writing family for teaching her. Thank you for helping me realize I know how to write emails, even when it feels like I don't. To Nadja Tiktinsky, for reminding me that sometimes I really do need to describe the setting. To my very own writing Jew Crew, Marisa Kanter, Rachel Lynn Solomon, and Carlyn Greenwald, for always showing up in the group chat. Seeing Jewish characters in your books and knowing that teens get to see them too means the world to me. To Kelsey Rodkey, Jenna Miller, Karis Rogerson, Khadijah Danielian, Alyssa Pugliese, and everyone who read this book at various stages, with an extra special thank-you to my sensitivity readers. This book would not exist without your insight.

I wouldn't be here today without my amazing New School Writing for Children and Young Adults team. Thank you to Coe Booth, who helped me solve major story problems on more than one occasion, Sarah Weeks, my incomparable graduate advisor, Caron Levis, the champion of all things writing for children, and Andrea Davis Pickney, who taught me to bring my twinkle. To my cohort, thank you for keeping "the riot alive." I can't wait to scream about all your future books.

To all those in the book community—the bloggers and reviewers, the librarians and booksellers and teachers. I am awed by all your hard work.

My friends! Hi! I know, I mentioned some of you already. But guess what, I want to gush about you more! Thanks for putting up with my shenanigans. From our European train trips to semesters abroad to "writing" retreats to absurdly long FaceTime calls, you are my people, my trail mix. Special thanks to Sarah, who made sure I had fun in college, Marisa, who makes the best matzah toffee, Sophie, for all the pictures, and Court, always and forever, darling.

Thanks to my family. My Becca-est Boo, I love you more than cookie dough. Sammy-Jammy, the dork to my nerd. I'm the favorite child. (It's in writing, so it's official.) Gunga, for her mashed potatoes and her love. Uncle John and Luke and the entire Haley family, stay weird and loud. Uncle Dudi, who taught me the family recipes. My silly Safta, who talked to me for hours about the Israeli dialogue and family history. Grandpa and Sabba, I miss you and I love you. Nona, who knows the best museum exhibits and has seen all the plays. Bob-Mommy, don't murder me because you didn't get the dedication. (You know how Mom is.) Dad, for every dog walk talk and beep hug, and Mom, for all the books. As little Haley would say, I love you both two and half girls and a flashlight.

And finally, to my readers. You are more than enough. This book is for you.